ALMOST FREE

ALMOST FREE

Chappy

Copyright © 2011 by Chappy.

Library of Congress Control Number: 2011910650
ISBN: Hardcover   978-1-4628-8962-4
               Softcover   978-1-4628-8961-7
               Ebook   978-1-4628-8963-1

All rights reserved. No part of this book may be reproduced or transmitted in any form or by any means, electronic or mechanical, including photocopying, recording, or by any information storage and retrieval system, without permission in writing from the copyright owner.

This is a work of fiction. Names, characters, places and incidents either are the product of the author's imagination or are used fictitiously, and any resemblance to any actual persons, living or dead, events, or locales is entirely coincidental.

This book was printed in the United States of America.

To order additional copies of this book, contact:
Xlibris Corporation
1-888-795-4274
www.Xlibris.com
Orders@Xlibris.com
101192

It was summer again, hot and dry and a beaming sun turning his shoulders dark brown. It was good to be home again. He had been gone so long, for him; he believed he would never sit in the old rocker in the back yard again soaking up the sunshine. Mike hadn't been home to stay in over three years but now he knew he was almost free. He could hear someone again knocking loudly at the front door, but it wasn't time to communicate with anyone yet and maybe for some time to come. He was in all probability at least ten years older than his natural birth age and felt older than that. When he was unshaven and his hair not brushed, like now, he looked many years older than he was. He was a lanky man, six foot three, and walked like a sleeping lion awakened too early from a nap would stride, always searching the faces of those he passed, and sniffing each as they strolled by him. Yes, smelling others like an animal would, expecting that strong odor that had been around him for the whole three years, a smell he would never forget and hoped he would act the right way if he did smell it again. To be sure he wasn't hunting for the odor, it was just a new habit and he wanted to be prepared to get away from it. The knocking on his front door had stopped and he was sure no one but he had a key. Not even the most malicious person would know about the private key under the cactus plant. Even if the person knocking knew he was sitting out here, there was nothing they could do except crawl over the seven foot wood fence now that he had a new lock on the gate on either side or come through the house. The back yard was inaccessible with large trees from eager people trying to find him, not to return him to where he had come from, but perhaps to try and console him into trying to accept the human race again without the bitterness they accepted he must feel. Of course he understood that there were some who probably despised him enough to attempt to harm him, but he felt safe here in his own back yard. He had his own apprehensions and didn't need to add anymore. This young man that had grown up in a conscientious family and having been a boy scout, a life guard, a high school football star and a combat Marine in Vietnam was now at a pretty discouraged part of his young life. Although he realized that the potent liquid in his guts was causing his depression, after last night he felt he could control it in the future. He couldn't conceive of ever being so disbelieved in his life, but he knew it was time to forge ahead. He owed it to his mother Christine Taylor who was a senior supervisor at the nearby nuclear plant and had more than one advanced degree with his father, Raymond, who was a senior professor of Science at the university. He had met Chris while working on his Ph.D. and jokingly referred to her as his little professor. Mike had a high-quality mixture of genes to use for making affairs better in this world and a lot was expected from him. So far all he had done was disappoint almost everyone he knew. He was the first born and just naturally assumed to be a continuation of the learning and poise of his parents. He had finished the big encounter. He was ready to start now; he was almost free to think now about the more important steps ahead to restart his life and right now a nap in the sun was what he had planned. His name was Mike Robertson Taylor and he was a survivor of the botches of mankind. He had been accused of a crime he didn't even know about and sentenced to prison for the rest of his life. They told him he had murdered a man and women one night after drinking all evening at Tony's cocktail lounge. The fact that something terrible had happened around the small bar was not in doubt as many police vehicles and several medical vans were there for many hours before and after the sun came up. More than one white coated man was seen there and when they left, their place was taken by many men in regular suit coats and others wearing the uniform. They measured this way and that, they checked the walls of the building next to the alley for something. They took pictures of everything possible, meanwhile being photographed by the press themselves. Curious people formed a crowd on the other side of the street which grew to be quite large and then several policemen came across the street with pen and paper asking questions of everyone. As most of the crowd would soon find out, they hadn't come across to give out any facts about what had happened, they were there to get information. Most of the questions were about if anyone had seen anything strange of different during the evening the night before. Several people were seen being shown to police cars where they were taken from the scene. It didn't seem to the crowd that they had been arrested, maybe just asked to come to the station to make a statement or something. Toney's was open, but not for business, the police were seen questioning the bartender known to most of the neighbors. Paul the bartender took several detectives out to show them the small shed behind the bar, and those of the nosy kind in the crowd strained their necks to see what was inside the always locked door. Actually, there was nothing in there except old mops and things penny pincher Paul hated to part with, but the police had wanted to look in there, so open it he did. Paul was just not able to comprehend what the police were telling him as he walked around the bar showing them anything they asked. He understood that two of his customers had been killed outside the bar, but he could not make himself believe it was that two. He gave them all the information he could and excused himself to call the owner at the emergency number he had. Still no answer. While not what a normal person would call a cocktail lounge, Toney's was perhaps named that in a tempest of dreams of having his own place, Tony had named it that and was now long gone but his nephew who now owned it never had a serious thought about changing the name of this little hang out with eight tables and a ten foot bar just to make more money. There were no facilities for eating in the whole of the bar. There were only facilities for washing or cleaning behind the bar and a glass washer in the other room. If you chose to eat at Toney's, it was snack food out of a machine. Owen the owner was well compensated for the little time he actually spent there, mostly collecting money and payday for the employees, and sometimes wasn't seen for weeks at a time by the employees. Even though very small, it was profitable to a point that if you were to close it, it would be a loss. His employees being the ever present Paul the bartender and general manager answerable only to Owen, Missy the waitress and sometimes when it got a little busier, Paul would call in Sue to help out. Missy was a very good employee for being so young. She was dark haired, on the small side and pretty. She was very interested in one of the customers and seemed to brighten up like a new lit candle when he came in. She also was the reason for many other young men to come in for a drink but she only had eyes for one. It wasn't that it was a big guarded secret or something, probably the only one who didn't know about it was Owen the owner. Not that he would have objected to it, but he did play the dart game with her love every time he could. It was such a place that there was hardly any bad talk or trouble from the middle class neighborhood, nor from the employees. He allowed Paul to take their weekly pay out of the till if he wasn't going to be there. Sue was a stout women jack of all trades and handled all incoming and outgoing deliveries for the bar. She might have been thirty five or fifty five, those who knew weren't saying and those who didn't tried to guess. When she came in for bar duty, she was good at that job too. When talking to her, you almost felt like saying yes mam, no mam. Owen would have sold the place long ago but he certainly didn't need the money, and figured rightly that the employees did. He enjoyed talking to some of the regular patrons. Often, when he did stop by, he would play a game of darts with a young man from the neighborhood that went by the name of Cholley who thought he was good at darts because his parents were from England where his father had been somewhat of a champion at the game. Cholley was a straight shooter with a little bit of a wimpy English accent even though he had been born here and had never gone to England. He hoped that Missy wasn't so nice to him because of his accent; he could learn to love that girl.

She was only twenty one to his twenty two, and he hadn't made it known to his parents that he was interested in an American girl yet for fear they might disapprove. He was not as manly as he desired to be and wished for the constant approval of his parents. Pretty soon though. The other people in the bar, having talked to him quite often realized that he probably got the accent from his parents. He actually wasn't too substandard at the game of darts, but Owen was an unrecognized master at the game and just didn't lose. He never played for money or drinks and usually bought the house a round when he beat another supposed champion. He was constantly being told he should enter large tournaments and win big money. It was hard for him to explain why he didn't need any more money, without admitting how much he did have already, and that was a no no. He was in his late forties and traveled the world just to see things he had been taught about in school, sometimes alone, sometimes with a beautiful lady he had once introduced to everyone in the bar. His uncle had been a dreamer and he had followed in his uncle's foot—steps also inheriting his money just like Tony had done. It was called old money. Owen had learned about darts when his father had run the bar, in between Tony and Owen. His father quite simply was a drunk and would have given away the place if the family hadn't stepped in. When he was eighteen and didn't want to go to college, he was assigned as a watchdog on his father at the bar, to keep him straight. He found it very boring and threw darts every night and day to keep from trying to control his father and became very good at it, leading to many matches in clubs in his family's circle. He was then given the club and a large inheritance when his uncle finely passed away. He now had more money than he would ever need and immediately made plans to see the world. It was a very good plan and he did work very hard getting the kind of people he wanted to run the operations he now owned. He cleaned out all the people his father had hired, at the bar and several little investments around town and actually set down one whole evening to drink and eat with Paul. He wanted to hire him as the manager/bartender of the little club, but he wanted to make sure Paul was the right person. He was pleased with Paul and gave him all the authority to hire and fire all employees he thought necessary, a great salary with the right to pay what he considered the right amount to any employee. As a person checking an employee for background information, he had never looked into his deep background because he didn't believe it was necessary to run a small bar. He would have been shaken to his roots if he had checked and found out Paul had at the age of eighteen had run away from home and caused a lot of pain for a lot of people. That he could leave on his own was no problem, he was eighteen and not running from a crime, but in not having any transportation to run away in, he hopped a freight train. Not long after he left town, his parents were visited by a neighborhood couple who tearfully told them their son had made her pregnant. She admitted that she had tried to come on to Paul when her husband was overseas in the service, and he had seduced her quickly enough. When she found out she was pregnant she first told her husband she had been raped by Paul but changed her mind when her husband was going to the police. Now her husband was trying to sue Paul and forgive his wife at the same time. It was complicated and hard to understand just what it was they wanted. It did look to an outsider as if the women's husband still wanted her but also support for the child that he had told the wife they couldn't yet afford. For her to admit she willingly slept with Paul and was now pregnant would seem to clear Paul from further duties as she was married and wanted to keep the child. Paul's parents were in a quandary as to what to do when they received a telephone call from Paul saying he was in jail in Florida for causing a railroad detective to lose a leg. This was too much to take at the same time, so his father said to the young couple" Do you see that door you came in? Well get out of my house, and don't come back". They quickly left yelling that they would sue, but he closed his door and his heart to the grandchild now just beginning to show on its mother. It seemed that Paul had been hiding in an empty freight car when the detective had tried to throw him off and in the fight; he had thrown the man off the moving train and under the wheel which quickly cut off his leg. Due to Paul's father, and his knowledge of the law, he managed to save his son many years in prison. He could have gotten twenty years hard labor; he was tried in a Florida court and sentenced to sixteen months in prison. After nine months he was released and came home to find his other problem solved as the couple had moved on, but left him with the knowledge that he had a son or daughter someplace out there in the world. His life was forever changed as a result of fathering a child and having no contact with the child. He maintained a strictly social as opposed to sexual contact with any women. Once he was married, then he reasoned, then he could have plenty of children. So far, he was still looking for the right women. He had been a wild kind of teenager but after the Florida incident he had grown up went to work and moved on when his parents died, ending up in Toney's Bar where he was quite happy as a respectable manager at thirty six years old. He was very good at learning from his mistakes and it was a tribute to his learning that he was now what most employers were hunting for in hiring a manager type employee. Paul was also a very lucky person that he was still alive. The story was that shortly after opening one day on a Saturday, two young boys, perhaps thirteen or fourteen came in the door just after he unlocked it, brandishing a small pistol and demanding all the money. He was in no mood for kids pranks with so much to do getting the bar open for business so he turned on them yelling "I don't have times for games this morning boys, so get out now" sort of pushing on them to leave. They left and not too long after that he heard a police siren, thought nothing of it and continued to prepare the bar for opening. He had completely forgotten the little matter until he spotted his always first customer, and decided to laughingly complain to him about it. His first customer was his usual one, Burt the going off duty beat patrolman in this neighborhood. Before Paul could tell him about the kids, he was sitting there having his usual shot and beer when he told Paul of the two young boys that tried to rob a gas station down the way and were caught with a real gun with bullets in it. They had fired at but missed the station attendant. Paul went pale for a moment and only after Burt asked him what was wrong, did he tell of his experience that morning with probably the same two boys. The temporary co-owner of Toney's, Owen's father was quietly retired to a nice quiet place where he drank himself to death in a short time and was forgotten even faster. As soon as it was noticed by the neighborhood that there was a new owner of the bar, business went in the tank because the people drinking there were asked to pay their bar bills which his father had illegally sanctioned and the free drinks were no longer given out so generously. With Owen's money, Paul slowly but surely built the business back. There were what you would call a regular clientele or semi-regular, but it was also a handy place for a quick drink with a quick couple of steps to catch the bus if you mistakenly drank a little too much. It was on a street with other small stores and houses, most of which looked like they could use a coat of paint. City laws kept the space between the houses and the bar at a discrete distance and it was open from noon to two am and painted every year, no matter what. Some of those regulars were Mike and several friends, Montel and Bud, who would show up once or twice a week depending on whatsoever. Montel had seen Mike's sister just one time and had fallen in love with her, no one knew about this and probably never would, but he sure wasn't going to screw it up by fighting or arguing with Mike and hoping for an introduction to Marcie. Both of them had been in the service, Bud in the Navy and Montel in the Air Force, and they were sometimes harassed by Mike for taking the easier service. Bud was almost thirty and set on his ways about his fears of getting married, had a good job, good pay and plenty of the kind of girls he liked, single and planning on staying that way. It was not Bud's way to worry about small things in life, he had enough to worry about with his tiny piece of the Chicago Cubs baseball team and other small business stocks. Montel always tried to agree with Mike after seeing his sister but he had been a crew member on one of the big bombers that seem to stay in the air forever and he resented being called weak. It wasn't that the big beauty was uncomfortable or too hot or cold, it just didn't have everything he liked on it, like pretty girls and good whiskey. There were almost never fights in the bar, maybe because the quiet way it was run. It was almost like having a drink in your home. There were no serious drinkers but some of the younger ones could get serious sometimes when playing drinking games. Although Mike was a very mild person and the most serious who never showed anger at those he disagreed with, he did have sort of a problem with his drinking, and was known to drink beyond a conscious mind occasionally. He had yet to consider it serious enough to stop drinking completely. He would have a vague memory of losing track of things for a short time after waking up some times but it always cleared up by the time he was in the shower. It had been and still was in his opinion something to laugh about or be razzed about and in the past he had been told he had borrowed money from one of them when he mentioned that he couldn't remember what happened the night before. He was serious enough about it to offer to pay their money back, but they would just laugh at him and remind him of something they were sure he would remember, and always he would then put everything together. This was not an every night thing; sometimes he didn't notice it for weeks. He also was not real crazy about his friends telling other people about it, as he felt defensive about this fault of his. Old Eddie had cautioned Mike regarding the blackouts, telling him to back off from drinking every night and see if it helped. Old Eddie was an every night attendee, skinny as a rail, probably about seventy five and a former jockey at many national tracks. He sat in the same place every night it was open, had four drinks of bourbon and water and left, talking to anyone who wanted to talk, but never accepting a drink nor buying one for anyone at the bar. He was about average for a jockey, almost five and a half inches over five, and about one hundred twenty six pounds. He was always warned about the wind if it was blowing hard when he was ready to leave for the night. He liked to remind young people about what the booze would do to you, sometimes admitting that in his younger days he drank way too much one night and rode a very popular horse the next morning, just after a little wake me up glass of bourbon. He won the big race, only waking up commencing with the flash bulbs standing next to the proud owner being photographed for the evening paper. Even years later after visiting many doctors about his condition, he still couldn't remember that ride. He watched films of it many times later and noticed nothing different from the usual way he rode a horse. Some said he was getting senile early, but after the story and others got out about his drinking, he was let go by everyone he had ever ridden for and retired with a small pension. He had also been thrown out for drinking too much by his wife who had put up with it for thirty years, so when the owners had let him go, so had she. Sometimes he would also tell you of many races he rode blind drunk and remembered every bounce on the tiny saddle, every piece of muddy track that hit his glasses and still be smiling drunk in the winner's circle. He wouldn't brag about his ability to ride drunk and he thought the world about AA. Even he didn't know why the continuance of the four drinks. He was considered a one in a million exception by some of his friends because he stopped drinking completely, got his health together and now never drank more than the four drinks at Toney's. He had gone to AA in desperate condition and after they had helped him, he grew into the four drinks thing on his own some ten years later. Benbe Taylor, called Liz by everyone and no relation to Mike, was considered a regular in the bar and hardly missing a night except Mondays when she mysteriously stayed away. It was well known that she went by the name of Ben everywhere else, but in this bar she was Liz, named that by Old Eddie after Liz Taylor. Whether as a slur to the real Liz Taylor, or a comical boost to Ben, was unclear. She was very nice lady about thirty five, and about three hundred pounds packed into a five foot two frame. When she laughed, which seemed to be all the time, she shook like a big bowl of Jell-O. No one knew too much about Liz except she didn't get falling down drunk and never had a harsh word about anyone. She had supposedly told one older man once that she had been married when she was very young, but was now divorced. It was not known what she meant by; very young. The big question to her always was what kind of name was Benbe? She didn't know about the name until she started school and the other children asked about it. She was always called Ben at home and later by her friends. As she grew older, she just assumed her parents wanted a boy when she was born and named her as close to her grandfather's name as possible. When she asked her parents about her name, they just brushed her off until she didn't care anymore. Her grandfather Benjamin left her a very large legacy when he died and she had banked it and gone to work instead of blowing it all. She had gone to school and become a pastry chef of all things. It was a glands difficulty, not the pastry that turned her into this walking bowl of laughing Jell-O. It would not have made a difference if she was three hundred or one hundred pounds to the people who knew her, they all loved her. Everyone talking about her and the murders outside agreed, she was the only one completely cleared of being involved in the murders; she was too short and too round. What wasn't known to her friends was the fact that she was actually thirty nine and had a ten year old daughter and supported her from the trust she had set up for her. She kept her hidden away in an exclusive school which she visited every Wednesday Morning and Monday night. She had never been married, but lived with a man for several months before finding out he was wanted in Canada for rape. That was just enough time to get pregnant and after seriously considering an abortion, she had the baby and was banned from her family home. She had never heard from the father of her child and didn't want to. She planned on some-day having her daughter and her move to California, then her glands starting acting up and she zoomed to two hundred seventy pounds in one year and changed all her plans. Now her plans were to wait one more year then take her daughter to a sister's house in Arizona, buy a home and show her daughter she was still the main thing in her life. She had her examined every month to catch any glands trouble. She had already explained to her daughter about her daddy when she turned ten years old. The only reason she drank at Toney's was pure loneliness, and she didn't want to be a drag on her daughter. She wanted no little momma's girl, she wanted a healthy, intelligent, daughter who would be an asset to the world. Regarding the murders that had happened outside the bar recently, the worst thing for Mike was he didn't know if he was part of that or not, or if any of his friends were, because the whole evening was a bewilderment to him, and try as he might he could not bring it into focus. He had never caused trouble in any part of his life, he wasn't close to being argumentative and he had many close friends who would swear by him. He was about as gentle as a former Marine could be. There was just no way could he be a killer as the police said he was when they arrested him nearby the crime scene. Even the police admitted there was scant evidence against him, but there were suggestions pointing toward him, like the jacket found near the bodies. He was respectful to the police when arrested, but had no memory of a murder or even of being arrested by the police. He knew when he work up the second morning that he was going to spend some time in jail and they had plans probably to question him every day until the trial. He didn't like what he had seen so far in there, but he didn't have much choice about the matter. He was neither sad nor complaining about his status because he had been brought up to trust the people who ran the city, and that included police as well. He asked his parents on the telephone not to visit him because he was ashamed of what they would see in this rough environment. He knew he could take care of himself in this or any place as long as he continued to think like a Marine. He managed to get used to the burnt toast, the watery soup and nasty warm coffee. At no time during this waiting for trial in the holding tanks did he seriously consider if he was guilty of the crime he was going to be charged with. As he testified at his trial, he went blank in memory at about eight that evening and no matter what the police or his friends testified to after eight o'clock that night, it was all new to him. His friends testified they sat at the bar drinking until almost eleven before leaving. Paul the bartender who had been a good athlete in high school and enjoyed talking to Mike about sports said that after Mike's friends left at eleven, he talked to him and the Campbell's until almost closing time. The Campbell's were an older couple who were also semi regulars. He stated that at no time did he seem drunk, did not spill a drink, and at one time, looked out the front window to check on his car. Paul, Bud and Montel all said he wasn't falling down drunk and made a call to the bathroom just before their leaving, walking in his usual way without a stagger. In fact one of his friends said to the other while Mike went to the bathroom that "That son of a gun can drink all of us under the table". The police testified they received a call from a tour bus driver named Glen that there were a man and women on the ground looking shockingly dead just steps away from the front door of the bar; Tony's Cocktail Lounge which appeared locked and no lights on at two forty in the morning. His tour bus group having been delivered home safe and sound plus a little bit on the drunk side a few miles back; Glen had made a stop just a few feet from the front of the bar at a regular city bus stop. It was his fault for not making a bathroom trip when he let off all those people, but they were all racing for the bathrooms at the club center, about thirty five, and he didn't want to delay getting to the bus barn. Then he didn't think he could make it all the way to the bus barn without going to the bathroom so he stopped in front of the darkened bar with an alley running beside it. This wasn't the best part of town to pee in an alley, but he knew it from when he had been a city bus driver and besides, he didn't feel he had a choice. He considered it an emergency and a choice of wetting himself and seat or an alley. He got off to take an emergency break and saw legs sticking out from the alley next to the well—kept bar. In this neighborhood, finding a person or body in the alley wouldn't be a great big surprise, but somewhat unusual. Glen thought it was some drunk that needed help and figured on putting him on the bus for a free ride to the bus barn in a better neighborhood to sober up before being spotted by the police. He walked toward the legs sticking out a little leary, just to be safe if it was a mugger waiting for him. What he found was a Mister Caldwell and his wife lying dead in the alley. He seemed to know right away that they were beyond help. After he called the police Glen spotted a man staggering down the street a block and a half away. He also disclosed that to the police when they arrived and they sent a car to investigate it. Glen had by now forgotten about having to go to the bathroom but he knew the urge would return as soon as he was cleared by the police to leave. He had never got used to seeing dead bodies even though he was a burial supervisor in the Army. He was the lucky guy that made sure everything went right up to the moment of burial, in Army burial ceremonies. It was a perverse thing with him, he didn't mind seeing dead people in accidents, but the person in the casket with all the flowers around and everything so quiet unset him to the point of distraction. When he got out of the Army, he stayed clear of all funerals, friend or family, but sometimes wore a little gold medal on his bus uniform that he received from the county from a nasty accident he had come across just after it happened, between a bus and truck and separated the dead from the living while waiting for the police. He did much more than that at the site, but that is all he would tell anybody. The completed file on the accident was a living testament to what good people can do for others needing help. Glen had pulled several people from the burning bus and laid the driver on the grass nice and neat when he realized he was dead. When he realized there were many people in the back of the truck, he carried or dragged the dead ones to safety next to the bus driver after giving what first aid he could to the injured.

All of the passengers in the truck were Mexican farm workers and were pretty bad off; the driver was dead and needed to be taken to the dead pile, as he was now talking to himself. He had called in the accident on his radio and suddenly they appeared from out of nowhere. He said later he hadn't even heard the sirens. There had been twenty three people on the bus and none of them were able to help him with this horrific crash. The nineteen on the truck were shook up pretty bad but tried to help. When the authorities got there they found all the live passengers sitting in the grass away from the fire with their various burns and broken bones and seven dead, two drivers and five passengers evenly spaced on the other side of the bus on the grass and Glen trying to put out the fire with what he could find. He was given the state life savers award by the Governor of the state, and a pay raise by the bus company. It was only later during the trial that he remembered talking to Mike in Toney's place when he had been a city bus driver and had stopped in on his day off. Mike had no memory of being hailed by the police car as he walked on the sidewalk. He was asked several questions which he did not answer and appeared to be sleep walking. It was a cool evening and yet he had no coat on and was shivering. He willingly got in the police car when asked to and caused no trouble at any time saying only he was cold. Meanwhile investigators had arrived at the murder scene and were busy trying to find out what had happened. The first thing they did was tell Glen to move his big bus to a better place so they wouldn't have to move around it during the investigation. The couple seemed to have been roughed up somewhat and there were bruise marks around her eyes. Temporally the stated cause of death was by strangulation and blunt force trauma. Their bodies were still a little warm so it appeared their deaths were caused within the last hour or so. The head investigator was caught completely off stride when he found her purse and his wallet on them, so they were looking for a sicko probably; at least it looked like that at first glance. Not too far away from the body and further back in the alley was an almost new black and white cotton jacket size 54L laying on the ground, nothing in the pockets except a pack of matches. When later in court it was testified to by laboratory technicians that many DNA found on the jacket including some of the Caldwell's, Mike's and the bartender Paul. The deceased couple was Mark Caldwell aged sixty four and June Caldwell aged sixty one. Both appeared to be in good condition generally excluding of course the marks on their necks and face. He was a lawyer and she a former dancer now a teacher of the arts. She at one time was one of the darlings of the dance crowd, beautiful and talented while her husband had been the lawyer with the movie good looks, never losing a case before he met June and only one after. Before they retired they lived apart only when they had to and travelled coast to coast on air liners so much they were know by almost all airline crews by sight. Later in court it would be shown that the couple was known to frequent local bars but was in no way to be called low-class drunks. Some said it was the idea of June to find people for local tryouts at the accommodations where she sometimes taught. She was a very strong lady and felt people that were relaxed and especially drinking among friends were the best at showing passion, anger and depression and that is what she helped others learn so as to make their dancing more unpretentious looking. She was thought of as a genius by many people she had helped, including some fumbling, bumbling people who found out they could dance after her patient way of instruction. She and her husband often approached different drinkers and she gave them her business card. They were known as well off and the husband once was a solid partner in one of the largest law firms in the area. It appeared that the husband was only there to protect his wife in case someone though she was trying to pick up men, because although he appeared to enjoy time with his wife he wasn't observed to sport a big smile most of the time. He wasn't a large man by any means but it was plain to any and all that to anyone planning any trouble with June had to go through Mark first. She was still a beautiful woman with a younger women's body at the age of sixty one. They had two grown children, both male named Robert and Grant, twenty two and twenty six, Grant became convinced that Mike was the killer as soon as he found out there was a suspect in jail and his name was Mike. It could have been any name and he would have thought him guilty. Grant, being rather undisciplined mentally and outspoken, made mention of payback several times in court. Most people who knew Grant wished they didn't. He just didn't have good relations with anyone, even his brother. Some said when they first heard about his parents being murdered, they suspected right away it was him that did it. Robert spent a lot of his time before and after the murders trying to calm down his hot headed older brother. He had still lived with his parents, but now lived alone in the large quiet house, when not in class at the university. Robert was a perfect fit for Mike's brother Cecil but due to the situation with his parent's death, he had never met him and probably someday would be able to sit down and be friends somewhere. Grant had married when seventeen when his girlfriend got pregnant and divorced at twenty when she caught him in bed with another woman. He had beaten on her every day of their marriage she was later to say to friends. His parents had paid his way through college and supported him while he wasted his life. He was living in a cheap apartment paid for by his parents, occasionally working to supplement what his generous parents gave him. He paid no money to his ex-wife for their child and recently had been sent a notice from the courts that he was liable for the past and future payments, and ordered him to start payments immediately, or go to jail. Meanwhile, the only suspect, Mike, had awakened from sleeping like a baby at the city jail after being booked as drunk on the street and a suspect in the double murder in the vicinity. He awoke with a terrible hangover which was not a normal thing for him and a big surprise at being in a jail cell and completely perplexed by the word he was also a suspect in a double murder. He didn't believe himself capable of murder under any circumstances; in fact he had been unsure if he could kill an enemy when he was in the Corps. He had dreaded the time when he would be tested but sure he would do what was required of him because of his training. When he served in Vietnam he once voiced his concerns about being able to kill with a friend nicknamed the {Flare}, a name his friends gave him after they were out in the booneys looking for a particular notorious double agent spotted close by when all they could find was one sleeping Charlie who looked somewhat like the guy. He snuck up to him and dumped a lit flare in his sleeping area. All hell broke loose as the man went screaming through the jungle like area, and fire was going and coming from all areas and sides. It took some time to get the friendly fire and enemy fire disconnected so they could get back to their lines. Flare he was from that day on, even when roll call went. Now Flare sat there listening to something he had heard many times from many people but now it was Mike his friend. He had met Mike one day at his shop in Danang scrounging parts for a rifle rack his unit had that was broken and useless. Mike had somehow arranged for Flare's unit to receive three new rifle racks, still in the shipping boxes from the world. He promised to take him out with him the next patrol they went on, but first he had to get the sergeant's permission. It was a sort of mutual pact, with Mike hopefully securing permission for Flare to ride on a helicopter for a normal run up and down the coast without getting off somewhere in the bush with other grunts to patrol some god forsaken piece of the country. Mike was no big softie, normal in every way, but even in fights as a kid he would not punish beyond a certain point when he got the upper hand and he was always big from the sixth grade on. He was also horrified that he couldn't remember anything after eight o'clock the previous evening, not because he thought he might have performed the murder, but because he felt so helpless not knowing what or where he had been from eight in the evening until the time the police say he was arrested. Mike had a major problem so severe, he felt ill when thinking about it and he had no idea of what to do. He only knew in his life of morality that if you were arrested, then you must be guilty, but he could not get his brain to think it through and present the deed as fact to him. He felt that if they arrested him, they must have proof he had done this horrible thing, but when they talked to him it was obvious they were searching for proof and a confession and couldn't or wouldn't explain how he did it. He had inherited many good qualities from his parents and if the police had shown him any proof he had committed this crime, he would have quickly told them all he remembered or knew, but otherwise as his father had told him many times, when arrested by the law, don't say too much before you get an attorney.

There were no weapons on him when was arrested, and he had no wounds, blood or scratches that he could see when finally awake and being questioned. He did not officially ask for a lawyer. They did ask him to strip and a doctor looked at his body from top to bottom, but said nothing and asked nothing. The only emotion he felt was for having a long blackout and the uncertainly about his whereabouts for so long. He felt that having been born with the ability to accomplish almost anything he had faced so far in his life, why now had he to even suspect why he might have blacked out for so long? He had never before had such a long blackout and after many doctors checked him before the trial, still didn't know the reason why. He was scared by one of the doctor's suggestion that maybe he had committed the murders and had frozen it out of his memory. When he asked how that was done, the doctor didn't have a clue, just something he had heard of in medical school. That was scary talk. The same doctor wanted to send him to a doctor who used hypnosis to find out the truth, but when told the results were inadmissible in court he backed away from it. He remembered sitting in an open air show feathering a show on hypnosis at Camp Pendleton in the Corps when a volunteer from the audience, a Marine he knew, was selected from the audience and strode up on the home made stage making all kinds of sneering remarks about the host being a phony and generally making an ass of himself before the host of the show dared him to be hypnotized. To the surprise of everyone in the audience, he relaxed and told the host he was ready if the host was. He then used hypnosis to take him back by stages to when he was a little boy after he was under. He talked to him as his father asking him to cut the grass, the audience watched him push the heavy make believe mower back and forth until he told him he was his teacher and many other people, even told him sad things so he would cry up there in front of everybody before he brought him back to reality. Before he woke him he told him also that ten minutes after he left the stage he would jump up and sing the first verse of the Marine Corp Hymn. When he was awakened he was shaken and angered at the host for trying to put him under and failing when he didn't remember a thing about the last forty five minutes. Of course everybody played with his mind, all staring at him and checking their watches as he realized something was wrong, He almost came to blows with those close to him, when he was reminded that when little he was afraid of going to the bathroom by himself, part of which came out when he was under hypnosis. While setting there wondering what had happened in the last forty five minutes or so, he suddenly jumped to his feet and began singing the Marine Corps Hymn as promised by the now laughing host. It was a long time before he was left alone by other Marines. Mike remembered from his time in the Corps about others having black outs when he was drinking with them, especially over-seas and they would do foolhardy things while drunk and when once again sober, offer to fight anyone who claimed they had done something stupid or illegal. He had never been accused of doing something he couldn't remember the next day. He accepted the hypnosis part because he believed in it and had seen it work but he also realized that his lawyer was right when he said it wasn't worth doing if it was unacceptable in court. Of course later at many cross roads when trying to find any secrets his mind was keeping from him, he wished he had gone ahead with the hypnosis, even if he found out he was a murderer. His father helped arrange a polygraph for him with many invited police watching from another room and he passed it with flying colors. He also arranged a medical bail exception for many tests. He understood the implications that although thought of as a big healthy man who was fun to be with, he might just be a homicidal maniac when he had too much to drink. Mike underwent various test and scans, blood tests, urine test and x-rays, and was found free of any defects that would cause the blackout. He even went through one of those brain scans where you have to use ear plugs or the noise would drive you batty. It is only about a half an hour long but it is a little trying on the ears. He had to determine if he was that type of person, but meanwhile there were plenty of people who wanted him off the streets and in prison for the killings. It was like trying to live in a dream with the scenes and characters changing every which way constantly. About the time he would convince himself he was a pure innocent person, there would come to his mind something he had done as a kid and gotten away with it. Like the bike he had been running from since he was ten or eleven, and how about the big spoon, his mother's favorite one, he had taken out of the kitchen drawer because it was the right size to build whatever it was he was building out in the yard, then blaming it on everybody except himself when questioned by his mother. This type of thing going around in his head made some think he was a little dense when they were trying to talk to him and he was caught in the middle of one of these fantasies. The newspapers had already determined he was guilty and should be in jail. Strangely enough, he agreed and didn't fight for his freedom, later explaining that to his younger brother who visited him at the jail, and wanting to understand how to help this brother that he was so proud of. To see the two together even if one was behind safety glass was to see twins if you didn't know them. His brother Cecil, being two years younger and working on his Ph.D. on Control of Nuclear Reaction in Space, Mike and Cecil agreed that if he was that type of person he should be in jail. Cecil was more about finding out about things, learning new things, sort of pushing his way into the how and why of everything. He also advised Mike what the parents had said; borrow some money from the parents for a super lawyer. Cecil was the very essence of someone who could change the world with his thirst for knowledge. When he found a source of learning something new from anyone, he stayed with it until he mastered it. When his brother was playing sports, Cecil was working on learning something new, and when his brother was out with the young ladies, he was studying for his university entrance exam. More than one person found out the hard way that he wasn't a wimp, gay or afraid. He was almost as broad shoulder as his brother and had also taken time to learn how to protect and defend himself. He and Mike had never had a fight going further than sharp words. Cecil couldn't do enough for his older brother even though the parents didn't think they were very close. His father had perceived this from his own bitterness at Mike for not being what he had wanted him to be, and told his wife that Mike was jealous of Cecil for getting all the good things that were originally supposed to go to him. His wife didn't agree with this supposition and for the first time many years, was angered at her husband. Cecil didn't make a big deal out it and if asked why he was so close to his brother, he was sure to tell you something like "Aren't you supposed to be"? Only one time was he put to the test of being the young brother of such a person as Mike. It was at a football game and Mike was having a super night as a tight end on his school team, and then as was the way it worked, on defense he was a line-backer. They were playing at home and one of the fans from the other team had decided to sit on Mike's team side. He kept jumping up screaming all kinds of nasty names about Mike and all the people around him, being loyal to their team moved away except for Cecil. When this clown saw he had scared everyone away but Cecil, he started in on him. When Cecil didn't say anything, he edged him on by taking his hat and throwing it down several rows. He asked him to go get his hat and the clown just laughed. Cecil grabbed him by the head with his right arm, and punched his face several times, threw him down, grabbed his feet and made him walk with his hands, pick up the hat with his teeth, then made him walk backwards up the stairs with only his hands. When they were back at their seats, Cecil made him stand up and apologize to all those within hearing of his voice. He was very quiet the rest of the half and moved back over to the other side of the field and started yelling again in the second half. As for marriage for Cecil, he had hardly thought of it because he knew what he wanted in life, what his father wanted for him and that only left time for wife thinking after he had secured his dream. His PhD was only the first step on his quest for the top in the kind of research about space. He absolutely had plans to be in space someday, not as an Astronaut but as a science investigator, sort of like a doctor making house calls in space. Very few of the people Mike met in the jail were people he would have had as friends. They all seemed to be bragging about their selves telling everybody that would listen how good they were about something but here they were in the same jail with everybody else. He found out right away that if you wanted to do something and they were in your way, you didn't dare ask them to move or they would attack you for being weak. You just had to tell them to get the hell out of your way or bellow out; Make a hole! And be ready to back it up with fists or whatever else you had. Most of the time, they quickly moved without saying anything. Some of the real bad asses would try to take others food from their trays and one dog eared old man reached for Mike's tray and came about an inch from losing his hand. That was only because when Mike swung the big fork at his hand he had missed by a hair as he was off balance reaching for some sauce with the other hand. He quietly informed the would be food thief if he ever tried that again he wouldn't need food anymore. He could tell from the inmate's eyes that he was on something stronger than aspirin. He was a fast learner and from the time he woke up about being pushed and shoved and thought of as a softie, he now was thought of as a guy to not fool around with. In all likelihood none of these fellow prisoners had any of the experiences Mike had gone through and if it were to be known, probably none of it would have happened. Everyone, from the man in the street to the chief of police were pushing for a; quick trial and hang him. Even some of his jail mates had read about him and preferred not to be friendly with him, although that didn't bother him in the least. He was caught short with money after paying the last three payments on his house at once, because he just wanted to get them off his back. There was no bank trying to do anything to him that don't happen to people all over the world. They were trying to make money. He was very proud that he had managed to double payment the mortgage very often and saved on the interest on the loan, but the bank knew they were losing money on him so they wanted to get some deeper hooks into him with another loan. He thought he should receive congratulations for paying his home loan off early; they seemed to him to be insisting he needed more security. They were not harassing him except trying to get him to buy more property. When he couldn't afford a lawyer and because of all the publicity he couldn't get anyone to defend him without a large down payment he made a serious mistake. Mike refused to take money from his parents to get a good attorney, mainly because he didn't think he would need one, and secondly he didn't think the charges would last through the first day. To say he wasn't warned would be an understatement. His family was desperate, even the turnkey advised him on the first day. Everyone was trying to get his head clear on what he was facing but he was in the tough Marine mode and could handle it himself. To him it seemed so bazar that here he was, a normal functioning man, completely healthy, having gone out for a couple drinks with friends and now suspected of two murders. He asked for a court appointed attorney and was given a thirty five year old wimp of a man who appeared to be afraid of his own shadow. He wanted to refuse but was told this lawyer, Walter Rinder was the only one available at the present time and if he didn't want him he would have a long time in jail to wait as the judge said no bail. He then chewed himself out for letting the looks of a person being the determinant factor in a relationship. He knew of a lot of Marines smaller than Mr. Rinder and bet himself that a good boot camp would make him into a great lawyer. He needed a lawyer to even fight the no bail edit. Walter was it. It wasn't so bad that he looked pathetic, it was when he had to perform his duties, he was woefully lacking in skills to do so. Walter Rinder was a strange person who loved the law but seemed to be too impenetrable to cope with all the complexities and little things you must know. As a child he had often played court games with other children and he was often the judge, district attorney or defending attorney. He grew up planning to be a lawyer and that was his whole dream. There were times when he was advised to take on reduced careers but he never quit and was proud of himself when he reached his goal. He was in a word brilliant in knowledge but had no other equipment to use with the brilliant brain. He was hurt bad when he was treated terrible by other lawyers but he failed to realize how serious his handicap was throughout the trial. This was his first shot at defending a real person and he was anxious to please everyone, which is impossible anyway, and just plain undoable as an attorney. Mike had no memory of that night so based on his own knowledge and habits on what he knew about himself and being almost positive he was innocent he didn't think he even needed an attorney for such a thing and let the attorney do his thing. It wasn't that Mike didn't care, this was his life they were talking about, but he was naïve to a point and didn't know about things in civilian courts. There is no great attorney in the sky to protect you from yourself in an open courtroom. It was an easy case for everyone in the court room except Mike and his attorney. It could have been different if he would have had any knowledge of the system, but he didn't and he had to pay the price. First his bail request was shot down when his lawyer sounded like a child begging the judge for something when he didn't have to beg for, and then his trial was scheduled far too soon to get all the things he would need to help him, he should have thought about appealing this harmful ruling as well as the bail ruling. It was pretty obvious from the start that nobody cared, respected or even liked the lawyer. He might as well not been there for the way he was treated by the prosecutor, and when he complained to the veteran judge, he was treated equally harsh. The prosecutor was a unpleasant looking gentleman that looked like he hated the whole world, and just barely accepted Mike's lawyer in the same courtroom. He was arrogant with everyone, but in the courtroom he was even worse, yet had gone to the best schools in the country. Mike had never met the guy's wife naturally, but felt sorry for her if he had one. Later one thing Mike made a mistake about the day before going for cross examination; he was walking in the courtroom with his guard, saw the prosecutor and said good morning. First, he looked startled then he leaned over as Mike was setting down and sort of whispered at him "Don't waste your time trying to butter me up gyrine,

I am an old jumper from the Army and think all Marines are useless". Mike just smiled and said "sorry" and turned away. Later, in the same day he was walking from the courtroom heading back to the lockup after the court was adjourned and Mike being a friendly sort felt the words "Good Afternoon", coming out his mouth before he could recognize the prosecutor as they passed in the hallway. All he heard from him was a loud groan. He wasn't that embarrassed that he felt bad about it, and he wasn't worried at what it could cause, he just didn't know any better than to be friendly. Hell; once while in Vietnam he had been challenged to box when the company got some new boxing gloves and the other unknown new guy was big as or bigger than him. He was under the impression that they were just going to spar around with each other and got knocked on his butt several times by the smiling other boxer. To say he learned anything from that was a laugh, he learned so very much that the next day he was challenged to box by the same gentleman, he tore into him like a monster from the time he entered the home made ring until the grinning other guy said OK. That is how he met the new First Sergeant of his unit. Mike was tried and convicted on two counts of first degree murder in an ordinary manner in two weeks' time as any right thinking man knew he would be, and his court appointed attorney did not rain any doubts about the police investigation, or lack thereof or on the powers to be. Attorney Rinder seemed lost whenever his turn came and many times, didn't follow up on things that were left open by the prosecution on cross examination. Mike felt like a prisoner of pirates in the middle of the ocean, and they had just tied him up and put him in a little boat to drift away. There he lay; staring at the sky and feeling sorry for himself for not realizing that they were serious when they had accused him of a terrible crime. Up until he heard the jury say guilty, he had been in a cloud like state and hadn't even thought about the jury sitting there. He had very little memory of the jury being picked, one, because he wasn't interested in something he knew nothing about, and two, his lawyer wasted any chance they had for acquittal by not challenging some of the prospective juror's beliefs that showed prejudice against him during the interviews. There was even an active member of an alcohol treatment center who made it plain that he thought the defendant was almost surely guilty, but should be charged with a lesser crime like manslaughter. He was not challenged because as Walter later said, manslaughter was better than murder. So there he sat, an easy target for all the people who thought him guilty, people who could care less about him as an individual and someone appointed to defend him that needed defending himself. Mike was only anxious to get back to work on his construction job and his life ahead. All the minor things about helping himself he had learned in the Marine Corps went out the window, probably partly due to drinking and trust in another person he didn't know and never checked out before his appearance. It just wasn't like him to be suddenly dumb to a point, but there he was facing the death penalty for murder, and not even seemingly trying to prove his innocence. Only at a later date did he even remember the older gentleman in the front row of the jury box nodding off every day when his helpless attorney tried to talk to a witness. The women who worked on her fingernails every day of the trial and over bleached her hair until it looked terrible sat on the end and never let a man go by without her toothy smile was another one Mike and his so called lawyer also missed seeing. She appeared to have more thoughts about herself more than any witness. The judge at no time called for order when people in the audience talked or laughed. Some of the security police standing around the courtroom seemed to be miles away from the action in the courtroom. They motioned to each other across the courtroom and caught the eye of the juror Maxine several times as she twisted her head back and forth trying to decipher the messages of the guards. To old time court watchers, the trial was a disaster because they seemed to be ahead of the defendant's lawyer, way ahead. Mikes parents were furious with his decision to not get a good lawyer, and his father had to restrain his mother from jumping up and screaming at the lack of decorum in the court room, and rightfully so. They were even talking about acquiring a court order to say their son was incapable of defending himself, and his lawyer was even of poorer quality. They were rebuffed by the judge and their son, and went hunting for a lawyer on the sly just in case they could get this sham of a trial restarted or stopped. The judge, known by most prisoners in local and state prisons as a man who would work all night and weekends to get the death penalty for a man convicted of murder, had wanted to send him to the death house to await the pain of execution, and he didn't know if there was such a thing, but one brave sole on the jury wasn't satisfied with the idea of killing a man who seemed to have been asleep during the crime and refused to go along with the others on the jury which required all twelve jurors to agree on a death sentence. Salvador Rakia was also an ex-Marine although he always told people who called him an ex-Marine that there wasn't any such thing, there were only former Marines. Salvador had also been a sergeant in the Corps and also went to Vietnam but as an infantry sergeant. He was a good leader and showed his love for the Corps and his troops by exposing himself to the enemy across a twenty yard dash, pulling a wounded Marine out of the line of fire at Phu By. He was awarded the Silver Star for this and if you didn't ask about it, you weren't going to find out about it, at least from him. He didn't want to get out, but the wounds he had received later on the same patrol were too much for the medical board to pass over and he was forced into a medical retirement. He wasn't even positive Mike had done the crime, but he wasn't going to let him die without some time to rethink about his misplaced evening. He would concede that the other jurors might have better reflections on why he was guilty, and would concede he had at different times in the trial felt Mike guilty and should be convicted but he was not ready to completely close the door by execution. He had been given many chances when he first became a citizen after migrating from Italy at seventeen and joined the Marines the next year to speed up his citizenship. He felt proud in the jury room when everyone except him was seemingly unconcerned about what had taken place in front of them and couldn't care less, impatient with rules, they were ready for other things. If the rest of the jury even knew how close he had been to fighting the nonvoting guilty verdict, they would have tried to listen to what he had to say even longer. Even when the jacket found near the body was shown to be owned by Mike, and he admitted it was his jacket and despite the implications, tried it on for the jury and showed it as a perfect fit, he still didn't have the same opinion that he was the murderer. Mike had no recollection of ever losing his coat before when drinking and he said he had taken it off in the bar and hung it on a chair. Salvador remembered many times going to a drinking place where he had been the day or night before to reclaim hats, jackets or gloves, besides It could have been taken by anyone. He also thought it wrong to eliminate the bartender as a suspect as he was supposedly one of the last to see the couple before their murder. The bartender had testified saying he watched Mike leave the bar together with the couple at closing time and Mike seemed ok, just slow and no, he didn't remember if he had a jacket on when he left and there was no jacket in the bar when he closed up. They, the Caldwels and Mike, were the very last customers out the door. They were friendly and laughing as he locked the door behind them, cleaned the bar counter and left for his car out the back door, neither seeing nor hearing anything strange in the alley as he drove out the other end. It was an unusual thing for the bartender to speak out about anybody, but then again maybe he got caught in the glow of all the publicity; or other motives. While talking about the murder, the bartender was allowed to say things that a normal defense attorney would have objected to vehemently. Like saying that Mike had spent an inordinate amount of money without facts, and guessing he was the one arguing when he didn't know who was. The pack of matches found in Mike's coat pocket was a mystery because he was a non—smoker, but his lawyer didn't even bring it up. No one was ever questioned about the actual time the bar closed, or did the bartender have to shoo them out well past two am. In the later appeals court, the lawyer was condemned by one judge as not only a terribly incompetent attorney, but a threat to society as an attorney. If the newspaper could have sat in on the jury in its three hours of supposed deliberations, it would have been a front page scandal. The jury never did, not at any one time sit all together at the table. A well-defined vote was never taken by the whole jury. The only time any vote was taken, there were only five at the table trying to convince Salvador to vote yes on the death penalty.

After it was assumed everyone said guilty on the murder charge and death penalty. There wasn't a big fuss even when the five jurors at the table decided that no death penalty was ok too. There were no questions about the case, and the only reason it took three hours to come back was because no one on the jury was going to miss a free lunch and one of the male jurors went to the bathroom and caught his zipper on the trouser material and one whole hour was spent laughing at his predicament and fixing it. The only thing they accomplished in that jury room was getting to meet new people. On the way out of the jury room to return to the court room, the foreman stopped the jurors and made sure they all thought the defendant guilty. No one ever mentioned the word innocent. If you were watching this with a secret eye, it would have looked like one of the older western town trials. As noted in newspaper accounts later that the lawyer broke into tears upon hearing the verdict. There were some that sought a hearing to determine if he was truly qualified to represent clients, but as always things kept moving and the right people didn't want to be bothered with undoing what they had done when he was qualified as a defense council in the first place. The whole thing smelled of incompetents on someone's part and they happened to be the ones to decide who screwed up, so the idea died. There was very little drama when the verdict was read, because it seemed as if no one really cared, and the members of the jury were gathering up their stuff, and the females were refreshing their makeup as the foreman was clowning for the newspaper before he announced the verdict. Mike was taken immediately after the trial to the jail below the court room and deposited in the large cell with other tried and convicted people waiting for transportation to the prison about two hours away, or so he was told. As Mike awaited his sentencing hearing and transportation to the prison he looked around him at the quality of people that would be riding in the van with him sometime soon and was pretty well aware that these were not the same kind of people he had served with in the Marine Corps. He had known many rough and profane people in the Corps, and even some that he was ashamed to call Marines, but there was a system for getting rid of these misfits. Mostly he enjoyed the companionship of other Marines in terrible situations where it seemed there was no easy way out but a way was always found. He was not in the mood for formal introductions with these horrible examples of mankind. He noticed that the jailers would take four prisoners at a time, handcuff them together and load them aboard the van. As they were handcuffed to each other and loaded aboard the van, an obvious show of non—trust for any of them. Mike found out about his sentencing hearing from his lawyer and it was five days away, so he relaxed a little and watched the other incarcerated people, Holy Mackerel; he thought; they can't all be this bad. His new neighbors at the prison were going to be hard to like. One new guy heading out that day was a drug dealer owing the state three years, who at no time would shut his mouth all the way to the prison, Mike was told by other prisoners after he had arrived, bragging about how bad he was and how many times he had been in one of these vans. One who called everybody sir was an ex-teacher convicted of having sex with about half his female students in a class at the high-school where he taught. The course name was Exploring the Unknown, and was looking at fourteen tough years in prison because as Mike found out, prisoners for some reason didn't like those who took advantage of children regarding sex. He was a smiley kind of guy that if after you had shaken hands with, you might feel like washing your hands, while the other two were a two brother gang that thought every bank was made for them and they withdrew many dollars before getting caught, they were heading for only a short seven years in the big prison. It was almost understandable why they were so screwed up at such young ages, when their mother had testified in court she said she had no idea who their fathers were and didn't think it was any business of the courts. It was shown that she had worked on the streets as a prostitute since the age of thirteen, and was dying of AIDS. They were twenty two and twenty years old. Their trial had been before and Mike had read about them and their mother while waiting for trial. It was painful to watch his parents visit him in the week leading up to his sentencing. They seemed so intimidated by the surroundings, and they didn't even get to see where he spent his whole time, they just saw the visitor's room. To say they were shocked at the hearing was being nice. The sentencing hearing was like a Hollywood production with the tough judge making the most of the spotlight. It was like the opening act of a play, building the suspense and the Judge, being a political animal with no big plans for the future delaying the sentencing until all the newsmen had taken dozens and dozens of pictures. Finely the judge decided he had wasted enough time, called for Order in the court and ordered Mike to stand before him. "You are one lucky person Mr. Williams and all because of some new citizen to our country don't understand our rules and refused to vote for the proper sentence of death for you," he almost shouted at him." Still it is in my duties as a judge to make sure you don't walk our streets again" he continued. "Your sentence for this horrendous crime is life in prison without parole on count one, and life in prison without parole on count two" he finished. He heard the gasp from his mother and a loud groan from his father. If the judge expected Mike to fall apart, he surely was disappointed as Mike had expected that sentence and would have fallen to the floor if anything other than the maximum had been ordered. Judge Stanly did not expect Mike to be surprised at the sentence. He had been around a long time, had sentenced many men and women to prison and had a dislike for every single one of them. He could tell from their actions during the trial how they would react to a sentence. He was just about to be forced to retire from being an active judge and was angry he was still only a lowly judge in a small courtroom. He had often thought of being a much higher judge, even supreme; lucky he was allowed to dream too. He still didn't understood why he had backed the wrong man for state office, but when he won and appointed another judge to a higher court leaving him high and dry in the city courts, it broke his heart. Mike was twenty six when he was checked in at the prison. He was a large man, six feet three inches and two hundred thirty pounds. Not handsome by normal standards but an open face with a perpetual smile made him appear softer than he was. His hair was short and had only seen a brush from birth. He had never married, probably because of how his folks always appeared to him as two separate people, with separate opinions on most things but not in an argumentative way. He respected them with no restraints, but as a product of them he was almost like them and did not see them as a couple who were very much in love. He also didn't want to be tied down with a wife this young. His parents had always been there for him when he needed them. They came to every game he played in high school and encouraged him to take an offered scholarship to a big university but he had other ideas and when he invited the Marine Recruiter over to his house to talk to his parents after he had graduated from high school was eighteen and didn't need their approval, but wanted them to approve anyway. He also wanted his coaches in school, scouting, and regular teachers to meet the recruiter. It was probably the proudest day of his young life when he was sworn in. He never tired of writing home about boot camp and all its challenges. He never once wrote how mean the drill instructor was or how bad the food was; instead he wrote beautiful letters about what he had learned. He even understood why the Drill Instructor was so seemingly hostile to everyone, he came to learn about the truth of soft living of forty or so soft kids the DI had to make ready for more war training in just twelve weeks. He had grown tremendously in general intelligence during his time in the Marines and then he had mistakenly branded himself with title of coward when he became scared in a helicopter when it was fired on by the enemy. At the present time he was a construction Forman in a huge company that didn't know who he was or anything about him other than his work history and ability. He went there to work shortly after getting out of the Marine Corps. He probably would have stayed in the Corps but for his last duty in Vietnam. He had tried for two years to get to Nam but when he did get there he was stationed at Denang working as an engineer when he wanted to be much further north where all the action was. He was typical as a Marine, thinking if there was a war, you had to be right in the middle of the fighting so he tried everything to get into dangerous action but only accomplished it on a piece meal basis around Denang. Being hit with rockets once or twice a month and running for the bunkers was not enough for many Marines including Mike. He was often on a helicopter as a passenger in payment for things he did for the crew on the ground. It was not an unusual thing to see other men and even women Marines riding as passengers on these trips up and down the length of Vietnam. It was not that easy as it sounds, you had to have a good reason, or have orders and it had to be on one of the scheduled runs of the helicopter. Most important, it had to be approved by the crew if no official orders were involved. It was called thrill riding by the crew and had few distracters. Of course those who did allow it on their choppers weren't shouting it from the roof tops either. When a supply man or other support type person was wounded while on a helicopter, it was quickly handled and unless very critical, the Purple Heart was not awarded or awarded later when it could better be explained what he was doing on a helicopter in the first place. Of course, all Commanding Officers had their own way of handling this problem. Most of the time he made due with minor jobs on the helicopter and once he was allowed to use the door machine gun on a suspected enemy troop concentration point. He could see no enemy on the ground, but was told that it was a gathering point for them. He had more than once been part of a landing team in emergency landings to help Marines wounded and no time to waste waiting for the Medevac chopper. He had also landed once next to what was left of an embassy office with several dead Marines bodies being retrieved by a Medevac, after the Tet offensive. Mike was mentally shattered when he became afraid when the helicopter he was in was hit with small arms fire while close to the DMZ but the damage wasn't serious enough to do any fatal damage and he was ashamed that he was frightened. One lucky shot probably from a captured weapon as their weapons except the AK-47 were not as good as our side, and you could get an argument started on that anywhere. It hit on the outside window braces by where the pilot sat and other than hearing the noise and jumping a little bit, he continued on his course. Of course to Mike it sounded like a bomb went off next to him for some reason and for some reason it became something bigger than life to him. He had never thought of himself as a coward but there in the middle of his being a Marine on his first tour, he was terribly afraid of dying. Mike just couldn't believe that he could be afraid as he assumed, just like a lot of people before him, that he was immune from fear in battle. The crew he usually flew with was a very good bunch of people, but they had to a man been scared when several months before, a lucky shot had hit their door gunner, killing him instantly. They recovered from the shock very fast, pounding the area on the ground with rockets and machine guns for some time. They as a crew were no longer nice young Marines; they were vengeful but disciplined killers every time they went up after that. The crew members treated Mike to a good laugh and made him an honorary crew member as they had seen many people scared in the rear of the helicopter in their daily jobs. They liked Mike and tried to help him. The crew later had an official looking document made up and presented to Mike stating he was officially a member of a combat crew under fire from the enemy. The strange thing about Mike and the shot that hit the brace, he would tell everyone that asked that yes, he felt like a coward. No matter that most people in the same situation would never tell a sole, it was one of the first things you found out about when you met Mike. Many other Marines had a lot more fear but were forced by circumstances to pack it away, and continue the march. That incident with the hit on the chopper took some of the lust for combat out of him mostly because he was now unsure of his ability to hold his own with other Marines. Then when he got back to his unit he was told two grunts were there looking for him and his buddies had found some ice cream for them and would look around the area and be back shortly. All grunts, short for infantry, were amazed at what was going on at the larger bases in and around Denang with people sitting in clubs drinking in civilian clothes, Air Force, Denang, people playing baseball and other outside sports and a PX that sold everything that a stateside PX sold, including new cars you could order for delivery in the states. Clubs operated everywhere and a bottle of good American bourbon cost two bucks. Big civilian jumbo jets landed frequently unloading and loading all manner of troops and pretty stewardesses coming and going around Denang airport. The two Marines were easy to spot as they walked toward him outside his workshop, how could you miss these grunts in the middle of all these clean uniforms and sunbathers. They recognized Mike from the information about him left by Flare. They were there because of a bond with all fighting men and those who supported them. They didn't look sad or depressed, in fact one of them was chewing on a piece of licorice when he told Mike that Flare had been killed the night before, and as they gathered up his stuff they found a note to go to the engineers find Mike and tell him sorry about that promise to take him out on patrol, he wouldn't be able to make it. Mike wasn't that bereaved about Flare because he was sort of supposed to die in war, and maybe Flare felt that way too and left the note for Mike, but he just wanted to go with him before he got killed. It didn't make sense to Mike either when he tried to explain it to a chaplain later. Mike knew like everyone that infantry {Grunts} suffered more causalities than other members because they went in ahead of other people and cleared the way for people like him, and the ice cream man, the whiskey man and the PX man. He always felt melancholy about Flare because he thought he was going to get killed. He had never mentioned it to Flare but he had told Mike on another occasion that he didn't think he would ever have the chance to fight in another war so he was going to have fun while he could. If Mike would have dwelled on this matter very much longer, he would also maybe become a patient himself in the sickbay. He was appalled at the waste he saw every day and he had no idea if it was only this war or every war. It was impossible for him to believe the tremendous cost of the foolish things he witnessed in

Vietnam. He sometimes worried about himself as a person afraid in a war, never to the point of suicide or something so drastic and when he returned home he forced himself to get out when his enlistment was up and became just another college freshman. That was another experiment he could have done without. After seeing what was going on around the campus, with all the hippies raising hell about the war. With the professors sometimes turning the class into a debate on the wrongs of the country for even being in Vietnam and the fact that he sometimes wore parts of his old uniform to class resulting in arguments with almost everybody on campus, he knew he didn't fit. Though sometimes he would admit the waste in a class argument, he quickly changed his mind about college and went to work for the construction company. For some time, he felt lost in the world; he didn't know where he fit in. He hated himself for being afraid in the war, and yet he knew he didn't fit in with the people against it. He thought it wrong for the people who were supposed to be teaching to be against the war, yet he had quit the Marines because he was afraid. He never made any bones about why he was hired at the construction office on his first interview, he was wearing Marine Corps boots when he walked into the office and the guy doing the interviewing was a retired Marine and noticed the boots. They talked for an hour, mostly about the Corps and he reported for work the next day. He started off as a pick and shovel man at minimum pay, but it was obvious from the start that he was made for this kind of work, gaining in knowledge and experience, he was promoted to foreman not because of being in the Marine Corps before, but because he earned it. Never before had most of these men seen a boss like Mike. He smiled all the time, he thanked the men for doing good jobs and he would explain something so that it was easy to do. Most of the crew were younger than him and just starting out when he was first promoted. It had taken him three years to get what others don't usually try to get until after five. He was very good at organizing the work day for his crew and wasn't afraid to pick up any tool to show what he wanted done. His crew liked him, his boss liked him and he didn't want much more than that in life. He had his close friend Kathy and they almost moved in together but for Mike's mother and her sensitivities to living in sin. They managed to enjoy a normal sex life without hurting his mother's feelings. Neither was sure they were ready for marriage at that particular time and let it run as it was until his arrest for murder. It was very hard going from a well ordered life working outside in the sun to shut up in a tiny cell in prison. It wasn't long before he was missing Kathy more than anybody. There was no huge prison yard with hundreds or thousands of prisoners, there was a small open to the air area for trusties and the lesser type of criminal. The biggest thing he missed was the smiles of people working as if it was designed to be a pleasure and not a job. To watch young people walk, talk wild and engage in horse play and accomplish tremendous tasks all at the same time was beautiful compared to the sluggish, unsmiling and angry faces he encountered in prison. It was almost like no one had ever told them about what happens when you break the law. Mike hadn't always agreed with what his parents told him, but he was raised good enough to know the alternatives, which a lot of people in the prison had obviously not learned. As a prisoner serving a life sentence and a new prisoner, He was allowed one hour a day in a cage like area about ten feet by twenty five feet attached to the prison, inside the wall, and if it was raining or snowing or anything that might cause the prison to shut down the area, you lost your time for that day, no changing hours or taking someone's hour, just; sorry about that. When he could, he would spend the whole hour just setting in the sun. Eating it up as one would with ice cream or something else that tasted or felt good. He never felt guilty about wasting his hour in the sun; it was like soaking up energy from the sun to get him through one more day in hell. He hated to miss his hour and would get a little touchy when he was prevented from enjoying it by rain. He had a very hard time adjusting to the lack of discipline in the prison, and had thought that the prison system would be something like the Corps, but stronger, instead it was terrible with the prisoners who really controlled the prison. No matter who or what controlled the prison, the worst thing was the general boredom inside those little cells. Many of the things good and bad that happened were because of boredom. It was well known to everybody concerned that if the prisoners decided to shut things down, they could. So called leaders were often in charge of many other prisoners and if they were bad, the whole group was bad. Most of the so called leaders were tough acting thugs who could get others to do their bidding by threats and beatings by other weak minded prisoners. It should be known these leaders were not appointed by the warden or other supervisors, but if one man with influence on a lot of people could keep the inmates in reasonable good temper, the guards would play up to him as a leader because it was one less place to worry about overall. By the same token, if prisoners were running wild and belonged to a certain group, that group leader was treated different than others, and was penciled in for harder time and constant scrutiny. Sometimes two groups would face off against each other, but at least in there, there wasn't enough space or freedom to have lost lasting battles. Most of the prisoners in this prison were lifers, but the majority was under thirty five years old, and hadn't learned how to live in a confined quarters yet. When the prison had been finished, they had decided to transfer mostly lifers and bad acting prisoners from other prisons. It was said by some of the first prisoners still left that the present prison was a playground compared to the first year when it opened. The old ones, as they were called, remembered many days when there were more than one murder of other prisoners. The guards had used a lot tougher ways to control the prison, and the guards seem to last only a couple of years before quitting if no transfer was available. It wasn't a good place to do duty or crime. It was said the warden of the prison had his own bodyguard when he went anywhere in the prison or left at days end. It was hard to find good leadership among the guards when they were constantly finding threats in places where prisoners shouldn't have access to. Narcotics were available after a prisoner had proven he was not a stool pigeon, at a much higher price than outside. One did not necessarily have to pay in money like on the outside, but could use introductions to another prisoner or your intimate body parts as pay for the right stuff. Sex was available for the right price, and there were male prostitutes available for the right bartering material. Although a big man, in his first month or so, he never looked behind him if he knew there was a guard walking as usual behind him, not so with another prisoner. You had to watch everything another prisoner might have in his hand, shirt or down his pants as he might be hunting for something he seen you using, drinking or eating. It has to be understood that a lot of these threats were just that, trying to lead you astray to believe this prisoner or that one controlled the prisoners and if you were afraid, you would do as told by these so called enforcers. In fact, it was true you could get hurt bad or killed if you weren't careful. Mike tried a different touch by asking other prisoners he knew who didn't play the game. To a man they all told him the same thing, don't be pushed around. Stop them from pushing on you before it became a habit. As he entered his cell block one day a well-known enforcer came out of nowhere and informed Mike he had to donate his supper to one of the other enforcers who was on bread and water for three days. He had never heard such crap since he got here and quickly wrapped his arm around the guy's head and beat his face with his other fist until he was holding him up completely and let him slide to the floor in the middle of the main hallway. When it happened, he hadn't even thought about guards but when it was over and still no guards, it became clear the so called enforcer had been left out to dry for some rule he had broken with the guards. It was funny, no one moved to stop Mike, or help the bully on the floor and after the hallway was clear, and he struggled to his feet and went to his cell. There was nothing ever said by anyone, even the guards who disappeared so fast that day. It was funny that the first six months he had been in the prison in a single cell lock up and it just about drove him wild to want to talk to someone. He had an hour in the sun everyday but that was also a non—talking area. Next he was moved into a single cell on the main floor and could exchange greetings or whatever with other prisoners, and walk to the mess hall. Finely he could live in a two man cell, have television, and go to the mess hall and the recreation room in the evening. God! He hated that place; every inch of this horror house called a prison was unbelievable to Mike. Of all the expectations he had when he knew he was going to a prison, none of them were as expected. He had heard many stories from older prisoners when he was waiting to come here, but almost all of it seemed to be on the questionable side. Especially about rules, who made them and who used them? Once when he was a kid in summer camp with the boy scouts, there were many complaints by the scouts about the rules and regulations of the camp. The head scout master tried to dummy down the complains by talking to the more level headed and older scouts. When this failed, he called all his assistants together and devised a plan for letting the scouts make their own rules for one whole day without any interference from them. A notice went out to every scout at the outing; they were to choose their own leaders for one day. Mike, being one of the bigger scouts became the supervisor in charge. He was just as rebellious as some of the junior scouts but he wasn't ready to have his first orders, and his last orders laughed at, and the other kids just ignored him when he gave orders to clean things up around the camp. Suddenly he started to understand leadership qualities, but he was known to everyone as the big guy who didn't care either, and he had to change fast to try to control these younger scouts. He found out very quickly that what he had shown as a rough young scout on the way up, had come back to haunt him. There were fights and some openly smoking their hide out buts, and when told to stop, ignored the orders. It was total chaos within a couple of hours and heading downhill. The only way to get anything done was with threats, and that was against the whole idea of free scouting. Mike would not bend and it was getting close to a big messy confrontation. Lucky for him the adult leaders saw what was taking place and resumed command. Later when he joined the Marines, he took that lesson to heart even though he found out later from the scout commander that it happened about once every four years and his command was one of the longest on record. No matter what the order was in the Marine Corps, he trusted it to be right. He now was among some crazed people similar to that younger time but most likely worse. His first thought after arriving at the prison was that he was glad he was as big as he was, when he witnessed two old timers fighting over one of the new prisoners, who was a little short guy about one hundred pounds soaking wet with fire red hair and the terror look of all new prisoners. He lasted only several weeks before killing himself with a dull dinner knife or bread knife at the table after being repeating raped every night by an older prisoner serving life. He just wouldn't be denied and the first blow hit his chest bone as he screamed and before a guard could get to him he had struck again and this time the knife slid in smoothly in the rib cage and entered his heart. He was dead before they got to him and the other prisoners at the table neither helped nor hindered him, but kept on eating. He also had been sentenced to life for being forced by a gang he wanted to join to kill an old man to prove his worth in the gang. He was barely nineteen when he got his orders from the gang leader to kill an old man who sat on a particular corner against a light post and begged for food. This young wanabe gang member slit the throat of the old man and watched him die on the street, was still there with the bloody knife when the police, called by a scared old woman, came. It mattered little who the murdered man was until the local newspaper found out he was a survivor of the Battan death march in world war two in the Philippines, down on his luck, too old to work even if he could, and bad health. Other young looking incoming men were bartered back and forth like a fish market in Japan, with the new prisoner not even knowing he was the subject until forced to accept the inevitable rape or acceptance of that way of life. That so many new prisoners accepted this drastic change in life styles was very puzzling to Mike but not something he had to worry about. Some homosexual prisoners came in with the idea that they were in hog heaven, until they found out some leader rented their bodies out to nine or ten men at once, all standing in line using the bent over newcomer like a machine. Mike had come across such pits of depravity once and the new homosexual had a gag in his mouth, his hands tied to his knees and blood all over his rear end. He saw no guard about and wondered why, but wondering in here he knew got you dead pretty fast. The bigger new prisoners were ignored mostly but given a once over sort of like buying a used car. If they were big, fat and momma's boys, they would soon be slobbering animals cleaning up after being introduced to anal sex or after beatings, performing oral sex upon demand. This was not an everyday occurrence but a normal thing many times when there were new prisoners. It has to be said though, with all the forced sex and punishing treatment that prisoners went through to live normal, the overwhelming majority used masturbation to stay on a level keel. From the first day the smell of everything got to Mike and all new people and stayed. The food, the other prisoners, and the guards were bad enough, but the smell was the thing that slipped into his sole and stayed. Many of the old-timer convicts or guards couldn't even smell the cleaner, but only because they had been in there so long, they were used to it. It wasn't the stink or stench of people, it was the cleaner they used to rid the prison of the stench and stink. It came in five gallon cans and was a dark purple/brown color and syrupy looking. It stank in the can, when you used it and for months after. When used on the floor, the thick syrupy liquid was poured on the floor like water; it sometimes looked like it had a life of its own, running between chair legs and splashing against your shoes if you were putting it down and anything in its way. Then the stinking oversized mops were used to spread it around equally, permanently staining the mop a terrible looking color only found in toilets. After one washing, in those big monster looking wash machines with maybe one hundred or more uniforms, top and bottom, five gallons of the cleaner added to the soap mixture and your clothes had the smell, and your shoes and socks, underwear, everything. It didn't seem to stain the uniforms the prisoners wore but lying next to a new pair it was obvious. Sometimes the new prisoners got close to a guard to smell his clothes. That is how they judged the guards, if they had on the same smelly uniforms clothes like the prisoners, they knew he was cheap and had his clothes washed at the prison with theirs. If he smelled fresh, they knew he took them home to be washed. What difference this made between a good or bad guard was unknown, but seemed important to some people. Of course many times when trying to smell a fresh uniform, they were mistaken in their intent and penalized for trying to come on to the guard. There were some men in there that were serving long sentences and had given up hope and decency, falling into the trap of sex with another man. It was forbidden but wasn't punished if caught and overlooked even when obvious. There were no such things as secrets in the prison, no matter how anyone tried to conceal something, within a week it was common knowledge throughout the prison. It wasn't so much that you couldn't go any place without running into it, but it was there. The prison itself was the same dreary existence every day, the same smell, the same people saying the same things to the same people on and on. Being in here reminded Mike of the fear he had felt when riding the helicopter being fired on and being scared, although he wasn't scared of the other inmates, he didn't want the fear or feelings of being a coward in combat to return in a place like this where it seemed that everyone was watching for a weakness in the other so they could take advantage of it. So far he had not met anyone that he would consider as a confidant in any way shape or form, but had met some people that a normal conversation could be held with without telling him they were innocent of the crime they were in there for. It was unlike being in the Corps where you were taken for your word, until otherwise shown. In this prison and probably all prisons, you learn that almost all people were wrongly convicted and the lies continued from that to every subject touched upon. So Mike fit right in, believing himself innocent and expressing this belief caused old timers to wink at each other and smile. These men, most guilty as charged, had the survival instincts of wild apprehensive animals after the first year and always it was; me first. At first almost all the other inmates left Mike alone, probably because of his size but as soon as they saw him routinely say he was sorry for dropping a sheet of paper as he was trying to hand it to a guard, he was a target as a softy. Such a small normal every day thing accepted throughout the world was considered something completely different in prison. These were all young men who thought to make a system of their own, away from the leadership of the old leaders, each trying to outdo the others with new rules and ideas. Of course he didn't know this and continued on his normal path and when he was accidently shoved or pushed he said nothing until he realized that it was becoming more often and took it to mean a test of his manhood. One unlucky felon who paraded around in self-made ink tattoos all over his body wanted to show his manliness to the other felons walked straight into Mike as he walked from chow, like a linebacker almost tackling a runner. Without saying a word Mike picked up the one hundred ninety pound man holding both of his wrist in his left hand, and grabbing his belt and holding him off the floor with his right, walked over to the wall with him and slammed him solidly against it, bringing him away from the wall three feet or so, then slamming him against the cement wall several times saying to the man he hoped this would help him walk straighter, and then dropped him in a heap on the floor. He didn't immediately move, his recently self-made inked ugly tattoo of Popeye on his arm was blurred and bleeding, he was wetting himself while fighting back tears. A guard rushed over to prevent more fighting by taking Mike to the Captain's office where he was given three days in the cooler. Later in the week two other friends of the felon were chosen by other backsliding prisoners to talk to Mike about his behavior with throwing their friend against the wall and; you know you can't do things like that without permission from one of them, and when they tried to intimidate him about it when leaving; Mike quickly jumped up from the floor where he had been doing pushups, grabbed the pair and busted their heads against each other while holding each around the neck and slapping them together like cymbals. Then he took them to the hallway in front of the cell and threw them out like you would a bag of garbage. The only thing that saved these two animals from getting badly hurt was the fact they had grown up that way and were used to being banged around. This cost three more days in the cooler, but he was never approached again in a nasty way by other prisoners who knew him. He was known to take no crap from other prisoners and the guards seemed to go easier on him than others. To him it just didn't make sense that people who lied, cheated, and stole everything that wasn't nailed down on the outside, raped, robbed and assaulted any one they wanted to on the streets of any city should now try to force a code of honor on fellow prisoners. He was big enough that even when other people were ganging up on others who ran afoul of their orders when disrespecting some self-made supervising convict edit, too many of the convicts had seen Mike trash someone in the joint and wanted no part of him even in a gang. One day Mike was called from his workout and told to report to the Captain's office guided by a punchy guard they called Wild Max because he resembled an old fighter everyone knew of and seemed to always watch as he seemed punch drunk. No one seemed to dislike Wild Max for some reason, probably because he looked like he was in another world most of the time. Mike always had the feeling though that he would be tough to fight if you ever got him to come awake. Entering the office with Mike as he tried to remember the protocol they had been taught when in that office and the ever present smack of the baton on the butt made you remember. The guard on duty as head guard today was called Fast Freddie for some reason, maybe because he didn't waste time with any formalities when talking to a prisoner. It was said that he once had to tell a prisoner that his wife had died and when the convict stepped inside the door, Fast Freddie shouted at the prisoner" She is dead, you killed her with your stupid crimes and time in places like this" then dismissed him without telling him who had died. The poor guy didn't realize who had died until weeks later when he got a letter from his daughter. Anyway, Mike was told that the courts had decided to review and determine if he had been fairly defended at trial and his case would be looked at and maybe he would get a new trial or his sentence might be reduced or whatever. He was warned that this would take some time, not to get impatient, and keep his complaints to himself. What he didn't tell him was that he was just one of thousands across the state to get this review and it might take years. Mike had promised himself that he would not believe anything they said until he was on the outside looking in, and he wasn't going to be awestruck with this announcement. This came when he already had eight months in prison and he settled in and tried to make the best of it. There were only six hundred prisoners in the prison and everyone, or almost everyone wanted out. Not tomorrow or next week or next year, that wouldn't do, it had to be today. This prison was built as a maximum security prison mostly for long time sentences. Even Mike wasn't that crazy, but then again he didn't know if he was supposed to be in there or not. He had filed enough appeals to last all year, but inside he realized that there was little else he could do as he was still uncertain what part if any he had wrought the night he was arrested for the murder that got him where he was. The system never stops, for Mike or anybody. While someone somewhere was trying to determine if he was guilty of a monster crime, life went on in prison. Every Wednesday at three in the afternoon new cocky people would arrive and every Friday at three some stooped old men would shuffle out the gate having paid their debt to society and board a free bus to the nearest town, free at last. Most never get out, whether dying by their own hand, as was quite common, or dying from old age or maybe at the hands of other prisoners. It was very hard to tell the age of prisoners so Mike came up with his own way of questioning someone about their age. He would automatically add an extra year for every year they had served in prison. For instance if a man forty years old looked about sixty and had served ten years, he would probably be about fifty years old or ten years older than he was. Only those who knew Charlie Tooms who was serving several life terms for murder knew that he was going crazy. Oh; Charlie knew it or suspected it but couldn't or wouldn't say anything about it. If he had talked about it, he would have said it was no big thing. Some said he was sixty five years old and had been one of the transfers in when this place had been built and he had served ten years before coming here. He looked much older than that, but younger prisoners who tried to push him around when he was among other prisoners sometimes got knocked on their butts. It just didn't make any difference to him and he was sort of looking to death any way to make an attempt of paying back to society for killing his mother and father when he was drunk and loaded to the gills with drugs many years ago, so long ago he was unable to remember when or why. It was said by other old timers that he was a very intelligent person when he came here, but time took its toll and now he was considered as crazy as most old timers. It wasn't that he acted so different than other prisoners; he just seemed to be withdrawing into himself more and more every day. The less he talked, the more he seemed to slip away, sometimes going whole days without saying a word. He was almost like a mummy to most prisoners. He had a better job than most people running the machine shop in the prison, but even now, his shop was being checked by the guards at night because of his withdrawal from a normal routine. For all the years he had worked in the machine shop, he was considered a good prisoner, but good by whose standards? The only one that was considered was the one the prison administration wanted. There was no way to deviate from the standards set by the warden. It was just not accepted, period. One day when he didn't show up at the warden's office to check out the key to the shop, he was found dead in his cell hanging from a homemade thin wire noose, probably made in his shop. Normally he would have been found when the lights came on at five in the morning or at morning count but a prison rumor said he somehow convinced the guards he didn't need breakfast and had told the guards he wanted time to be by himself. He didn't want anybody interrupting him for a while. It was also known that he had made certain creations in his machine shop for the same guards. It was not like anybody was shook up or anything; the biggest thing was getting another prisoner to replace him in the machine shop and quickly taking custody of the hanging creation before too many people had a chance to see it. Charlie had been a prisoner with a number, he was now dead. Finish. In this type of surroundings there was no time for grief or sadness from the prisoners or the people who ran the show. The very first thing that they thought about was a replacement for Charlie, and this started before Charlie ever left his sell for the last time in a body bag. This required some study of the records of the prisoners. It had nothing in the world to do with anything other than the safety of the prison because of the caliber of machines in the shop could fabricate almost any type of weapon. Being fair or impartial in the selection of the new machine shop operator was not even thought of. This was an assignment by the warden, not to be refused for reasons of the prisoners, but using a bit of good thinking on what could happen if you put the wrong person in the shop, more care was used in replacing a prisoner in that shop. This shop was never intended to be there in the first place. It had been there as a part of the construction of the prison twenty one years ago and was about to be torn down after the prison was built. From this shop had come all the steel reinforcing throughout the prison, all the steel bars on the doors and every steel beam supporting the roof, all of them had been delivered to the site and made to order on the machines in the shop. When some noble member of the ruling party in the state capitol recognizing that it might be a good way to teach a meaningful job to some inmates, he prevailed when they started dismantling it. There were still people around that knew about the deal and they just laughed at questions about this sacrifice the tax payers had paid an extra one million for the machine shop, none of it ever getting near the state treasury. They had trouble from the beginning, as the first two were caught making shanks and other weapons. The first guy to run the machine shop was a complete loser with several escape attempts before he got here. He liked being called Mister, and had it made his official name, thereby forcing the guards to either call him mister every time or his number. Another name he was known by in there was looser. He had killed a guard in a jewelry store he was trying to rob, because the clerk he was manhandling wasn't fast enough opening the jewel case. With a pistol openly displayed and people walking on the street heard the shot stopped in front of the open door of the store and huddled afraid to go in, and Mister too afraid to come out until a beet-cop ran up drew his weapon and ordered him to come out. He received a life sentence without parole. He was a rare spectacle, and never should have been trusted with the machine shop. He finely made one too many shanks that injured one too many guards or prisoners and was shipped out to another unlucky prison. The present warden would not even let his name be mentioned when he took over, long after Mister was gone. When he read how the machine shop was run, he threw a fit that every guy in the prison, prisoner or guard and kitchen boss heard how it was to be run in the future. Mister had scraped by for three years in the machine shop before being caught violating the work rules. Arnie Bush next held the job for five years before being caught making weapons for one family of prisoners called the Chucks. Arnie was also doing life for murder, but had a chance for parole, was the first and only person to run the shop and having experience with all the equipment in there before he got caught building the army of Chucks, during his fifth year. Arnie was a very well educated man, having studied at some of the best schools and had a very good hobby of working on all sorts of metal lathes. Having become frustrated with the academic side of life, he retired very young and opened a machine shop, doing so well he had no time for his family. Soon enough his wife found a lover and shortly after that Arnie caught them together and killed her. Her fleeing lover told police and Arnie was given life in prison. Charlie who was appointed shortly after George Garter was selected as warden and had been the savior of the program and lasted thirteen years before his memories of what got him sent there were just too much to carry any longer. It was a fact that by now, mostly because of Charlie, the prison couldn't afford to shut down the shop as it did more than pay for itself every day, and with an ever smaller budget for the prison, that was like catching cancer. The warden trying to outthink the state government decided that if he requested that the shop be removed or overhauled they would do the less expensive thing and close it. To his horror/ surprise, they had replaced all the machines with newer ones. So much for short budgets. After that, he never hesitated ordering anything for the prison. Now the thought was just maybe they could use this prisoner Mike Taylor as a replacement for the inmate recently dead by his own hand after thirteen years of good work in the machine shop, he was {interviewed} questioned by several civilian instructors brought to the prison from the industry and the head guard, and after checking out the entrance card each prisoner had filled out when starting his sentence and talking to the prisoner about it and offered [assigned} the job. They all agreed that from talking to him, they knew his big personal problem to be the self-professed statement that he was a coward in the Marines because he had become frightened when the helicopter he was riding in was hit by enemy fire. They also realized that they were not equipped to make him understand the unreasonable penalty he had given himself for wanting to participate in a war. They chose to disregard his silly belief and assigned him to the position. All this information was presented to the newly selected warden taking over when Carter retired. His name alone brought back memories to those who had been aboard some of the ships he had commanded for thirty years before retiring from the Navy. Andrew Necis was a strong believer in everybody doing their job without waiting for orders. He liked a smooth running prison just like he ran his ships, and when all his immediate staff was gathered for the first time, he made it clear what he meant. "If we have an assignment to make and it is important enough that I have to make the decision who or what happens, I will expect a recommendation from the majority on my desk before the decision is due". "If it is just a prisoner assignment, work it out among yourself before I see it and be damn sure on your decision, because I will sign it as is." He looked at all his advisors with a tough looking grin on his face and continued" I don't like to be embarrassed in front of my boss and the last one who did it is probably still serving about a garbage scow off Okinawa." All paperwork concerning who was going to be running the machine shop was withdrawn from the warden's desk and all five of the staff that had the job described by the warden, worked another hour on it and still came up with Mike Taylor. Upon reentering the warden's office, the chief of staff placed the recommendation in his incoming basket and started to leave. The warden said "hold it" took the paper and without looking at it signed it and handed it back. Mike immediately welcomed the job and loved being alone in his shop, where no one could come, not even the guards if they didn't get a key from the warden's office. He turned out tools for the prison and different gadgets for the warden and other officials of the prison. Somehow Charlie and the prison system had made a latch like piece of metal that was very helpful in the painting trade and was wisely copyrighted by the warden for the state. This particular prison received a good monthly stipend from the state to help run the prison beyond what they would normally receive. The money received supposedly strictly for the machine shop. He was now responsible for several almost new machines that old Charlie had loved to run and repair for the whole time he spent in there. He could play a radio Charlie had left, but not too loud and take a break when he chose. It was a nice job and wanted by many prisoners, so when he was assigned the job, he lost some more so called friends who had been there longer and thought they deserved the job more. It didn't bother Mike, just like it didn't bother him when he had been promoted ahead of other people in the Corps when he tried harder, did more, and improved his body and mind to the Marine Corps way of thinking. This was the one place in the prison where things had to be watched closely, as beautiful tools were made here and what is a weapon if not a tool. It was a closely watched operation by the administration of the prison. They had watched old Charlie very closely but never found him making anything he hadn't asked the warden for permission to do. That he made things for different guards was overlooked quite readily. Although he had a quota of different tools to produce, Mike had plenty of free time to study books on the procedures of producing different tools or other things. He took to the job and was actually proud when he produced something useful, even if it was to be used to control the prisoners, including himself. He noticed right away that Charlie had stopped cleaning the machines; probably they hadn't been cleaned since he felt himself sliding down the slippery slope of life. Mike asked for and was given one month to disassemble and clean the machines with little or no supervision. It was an amazing experience as he had never laid eyes on some of the machines before and as he disassembled and later reassembled them, he learned all about them, where they needed oil more than another place and what to do when they broke down. He completely lost himself in this venture and hated to be bothered when he stripped another part off a machine and realized what that part did or didn't do. Many days he begged off going to lunch when it was mandatory with promises of gadgets once the machines were running again. He cleaned the floor with shower soap instead of that offensive smelling stuff in the rest of the prison, to keep his machines from getting stinky. Just the sound of the newly cleaned and oiled machines turned him on, it was even scary to him. Mike used it like a crash course in mechanics and he loved it enough to forget for a while that he was in prison. It was almost like going to work at a construction site on his regular job. He became familiar with the machines enough to treat them kindly when they acted different, and check them over until he found what was wrong. He babied them and talked to them like little children, and even got on himself one day for going overboard about the job. The hard part of the job was turning in the keys every day at five in the afternoon. If it hadn't been for the smell in the prison, and everybody dressed the same, Mike would have forgotten he was in prison. As in every prison there was talk of escape, but most of it was just that, talk. Then there were people like Levi Evil, a self-named prisoner whose real name was Levi Turner serving a life sentence for murder and trying to hide his cleverness behind the veil of craziness so as to cover his escape plans that never seemed to materialize when needed. He had killed his wife in a rage for serving the same meal two days in a row. He had been in other prisons and was well known as someone to watch, having been caught many times in planning some stupid plan to escape. Friendly guards had told some of the better prisoners that Levi had been sent to three different prisons in a two year time span for grandiose escape plans that had gotten four other prisoners killed. He was serving life, but they kept adding more years on to his sentence and transferred him to another prison so often that he was a lifetime prisoner, with sentences to be served in three other counties if he ever made it out of this prison. However now he had what he said to be a fool proof plan to escape with twenty men at once and leave the local police at a loss for several hours while the prisoners went in every direction, each on his own. Some to be caught and given more time, but having the same chance to maybe be one of the lucky ones and setting safe in Mexico sipping a rum drink while ogling all the young beauties on the beach. There was only one thing stopping Levi and the rest of them from getting it done, and that was they had to go through the machine shop Mike commanded to get into the next shop where one of the wanabe escapees had already supposedly started on a tunnel toward what he believed to be the outside. This shop had been shut down recently for a new organization shop to work with prisoner's families. It was going to be a shop where inmates made Christmas gifts and other things for their children by paying a small sum for material and drawing the toy, their own creation, and the prisoner in charge and two helpers would fabricate the toy and if the warden approved it, the prisoner could then give it to his child. This was thought to keep the family together a little bit. The man, Micky, working on the tunnel had already put almost three months in digging the tunnel before the shop was closed to remodel it for the new prisoner's family work project. He had bragged to Levi that he had dug the tunnel almost to the outside. Unknown to the digger and the goofy Levi, their so called tunnel had been found after someone, probably Charlie, had reported it. The escape through that attempt of a tunnel would have been impossible by any standards. The shop had been making plastic cups before becoming the family help shop, The quality of the cup had become very poor in the last couple of months or so, breaking very easily and there was an inside investigation. That is when they found the prisoner Micky making the cups for the last two years had started mixing a dirt gravel mix with the plastic for the prison cups. Evidently the convict would put the ingredients for the plastic mix in the huge cement mixer looking tub, set the heat and when it got to bubbling and ready to boil, throw a bucket of dirt and stones into the mix and stir it in. The guilty party was found but left in place until the upcoming regular closing to retool for the toys. They knew from the looks of the hole in the wall plan that Micky was incapable of doing it alone. They also were waiting to see what others were involved. It wasn't hard to figure out how he was getting the sand and gravel; they just had to find where he was digging. It wasn't very hard to find the hole behind the oven with a cup rack covered with a sheet hiding the hole. It was just about big enough for one man to crawl into, and there was the rock, dirt and gravel wall facing them. It didn't take a genius to figure out that inmate Micky had dug only five or six feet into the inside wall of the prison, and headed for the main wall about a hundred feet away, and under the small yard inside the wall. They figured that with the tools they found in the tunnel, two large soup spoons, a one gallon empty can and a rusty eight inch screwdriver, it would have taken at the minimum three years, working eight hours a day to even get to the outside wall of the prison which was four feet thick at that point and filled with sensors every foot or so that would have told the warden exactly where they were. Oh yea! And having made a zillion more defective cups nobody needed or wanted. On top of that, if they had gotten through the walls without being caught, they would have come out so close to a guard house, the guards would have heard them coming weeks before they would break through the wall. They were within days of charging several convicts for trying to escape when they realized it was better to let it simmer more. Guards hear rumors too, and they knew there were more people involved. The warden had to get tough with some of his guards who thought the whole escape was hilarious and were about to be overheard by making jokes about it. Between each shop was a solid wall made of brick and steel that would have to be breached from where Mike worked into the now closed shop. These walls were basically like conventional walls but steel was substituted for two by fours and cement for plaster board, with the steel beams being closer together than normal two by fours. The company that built the room had built a fortress for the future, with the ceiling at nine feet and three walls facing the door having steel beams about every eleven inches and welded to the room above and below indicated that they wanted to keep their machines safe and never had any intention of removing the machine shop when finished with the prison. No other room in the prison had such escape proof makings. To some inspectors who later checked it, in their opinion the people on the machines making the beams probably made a serious production mistake and to hide it, they put them in the walls of the room they were made, never thinking the mistake would be found. Of course all this was in the blue prints, but what warden reads them or knows where they are kept. Mike worked alone behind a self-locked door that he had to get the key for every day and turn it in at five pm every working day. He was the only man allowed to use the key and he was warned everyday about using it wrongly. The plan was bold and self-serving in that there would be no escape for Mike as he would have to be there to turn the keys in at five to keep the escape silent and the pack of desperate men could not get started until four pm and needed the time to breach the wall, finish the digging and be on their merry way before being announced as escaped prisoners. Mike of course would be charged with aiding the escape, losing this nice job and extra time in the cooler. He was begged, threatened, and promised death if he wouldn't go along with the escape and let the men into his shop. He even tried explaining to Levi that even if he did let them in his shop, they didn't have the right tools to breach the wall, and he had no idea about the strength of the wall, or time for them to get outside before bed check. That their noise breaching the walls would wake up half the prison is something that Levi had never thought about, let alone the truth about the tunnel. Rather than think of some other way to escape, he continued to demand that Mike help them by unlocking his door. This was only days after he had been informed about the possibility of an early release or new trial and there was no way he was going to be part of a wild plan like that and throw away his future. That he had to maintain his companionship with other prisoners as not being called a snitch he had to refuse by himself of telling anyone about the planned escape and just not open the door. As the escape date got closer, the pressure became more intense, even from those not involved in the escape but knew of it and just wanted the prison embarrassed by the escape. More than once Mike was informed how hard life could be in prison if he didn't go along, but he always stared them down and said "anytime, anyplace" to their threats of a beating by one of the big mouth lifers. It went down on a Friday with only four of the twenty showing up at the door to his shop demanding he let them in, the other sixteen having chickened out after talking to Mike and others. He heard the commotion outside his shop door and looked out to see Levi, a large black guy he didn't know, and two sorry looking prisoners he had never seen before huddled against his shop door begging to be let in. Levi had a pair of pliers, the giant black guy had a shank about two feet long and each of the other guys had rags hanging from their pockets but nothing in their hands. Mike had a vision of these four losers attacking just the wall between the shops and as desperate as they looked and as serious as the situation was, he had to laugh. He just walked away from his barred windowed, four inch thick door and began his work amid all types of threats and demands being yelled at him, which pretty soon brought the guards down and trapped the four men in a hallway trying to get into the metal door of the machine shop, and no way to retreat. None of them would say anything, especially about an escape and Mike refused to admit even knowing about the escape plan and each of the four got off with threatening Mike instead of attempted escape and sent back to their cells with three days in the cooler for the offence. The regular population of prisoners greeted the news of the so called threats against Mike with no talk of an escape attempt with laughter and soon was playfully punching Mike on the shoulder when passing him in the prison great walk ways on the way to chow. Over the next several months, those four prisoners were transferred to other prisons one at a time with no fuss. The one thing that made Mike remember the incident was the clanking sound of the shank as the big guy threw it to the floor when he saw the shot guns the guards had pointed at them. It must have weighed at least four pounds. With that you could destroy the whole prison, given enough time, but the noise would be tremendous on the inside. The mess hall was always the place where you were eyeing and being eyed by other prisoners. There were always extra guards in and about the place because of the frequent fights between two groups of people, maybe black and white, maybe Chicano against the blacks or both of them against the whites. Sometimes it would be a territorial dispute between different factions of same race groups. Mike came to the mess hall only to eat and when he sighted a mixed colored felon heading for him as he entered the mess hall, he knew it meant trouble. He didn't know him, but you didn't have to know someone to get killed in there. Chucu, a mixed Indian with the blood of many races flowing through his veins was on a mission to kill someone but he was so drugged up he hadn't followed instructions on who it was he was supposed to kill. All he could remember was tall white man at second hour lunch time. When he spotted Mike, his mind, clouded with a powerful drug, he went right at him. He had that thousand yard stare and seemed to be stoned out of his mind. As he got to within six feet or so, he pulled a large handmade blade from his shirt and tried to separate Mike from his head. On the outside when you are attacked with a knife, very few people will try to help you for fear of the knife, but inside this prison at least, no one, zilch, nobody including guards would jump in to help. The guards might shoot, but more times than not they were afraid of killing someone else. Mike had learned this and did the best to defend himself. As he reached for a chair, the madman swung the blade at him and cut a nice piece of shirt off his collar, plus a piece of wood from the chair big enough to use as a club, if you could get at it, with Mike falling to the floor. Suddenly he was on his feet charging the knife man, knocking the knife out of his hand and grabbing the man by the neck, shaking him like a rag doll and flinging him on the floor like a young child might do to a doll. Mike seemed to recover himself quickly and waited for the guards to take him to the hole. He was pleasantly surprised when they told him to eat his meal and get back to work. They then had the attacker hauled away to the hospital. Mike was never told any more about the man who tried to cut his head off, but prison rumors said he had been sent after Mike by mistake and was now in solitary confinement until a decision could be made about his ability to mix again with the regular prisoners. Sometimes these kind got long stretches in the cooler, but most of the time they would put him in the cooler, wait a day or so. Then bargain with him with threats. What they wanted was the source of the drugs or booze he was on when the attack took place. It was no longer a big thing to Mike that some nut would try to kill him, it seemed to happen to everybody that spoke their mind in this prison. Everybody had to worry about other prisoners or guards they had ticked off who might want to get even for an embarrassment in front of a gang leader, or close confidant. Sometime all it took was a guard to look the other way at the right moment, when trash or homemade poison was put in some food, evidence of escape plans planted in another's cell or the worst, a homemade knife was quickly shoved into an unsuspecting body. Mike ignored the fact that other prisoners were talking about how he was able to recover so fast from the knife blow that almost cut his head off. He himself didn't have any idea or memory of getting off the floor and almost strangling the assailant. It wasn't an unpleasant thing to remind him that again he had looked like he had lost control when getting up fast. He was without doubt unafraid of his ability to get off the deck and take action. He was thankful he had the ability to do this and what would that have to do with killing two people he liked and were three times his age. He had learned a long time ago that when you are knocked down, you get up and knock the other guy down. Time was flying past and now Mike had been in prison for one year and still no word on his supposed early out or new trial. It was getting harder to play the game for Mike and he was threatened with the cooler a couple of times when raising his voice in discussions about the court. Through his actions in the escape thing, he was now treated with respect by the other prisoners, and some of the officials tried to help his cause in getting the action started in the retrial. The local press became involved with his case and was soon picked up in the big newspapers and the TV networks. He was asked by all of the major news companies for filmed interviews and told them all the same thing, go see the man. The Man, Warden, wouldn't even consider letting it happen and Mike stayed away from the whole mess. He watched old pictures of himself flash on the nightly news on his TV he shared with another man. When he saw the pictures he realized how much he had changed in a short time. He had grumbled the last time he got clean clothes because they seemed so loose, now he could see he had lost a lot of weight since being sent here. He and his cell mate didn't talk that much as was common with prisoners who were first pared off because nobody wanted a snitch as a cell mate, and sometimes it took a while for the snitch to get caught. So some prisoners thought the whole time that each other was a snitch. He learned that most long time criminals had all kinds of past deeds they had done, but never been caught for, but were in the prison for another crime they had been convicted of. If they were suspected of committing a major crime such as murder, it wasn't unheard of that they would get an undercover cop or another prisoner to find out if the man was the murderer they had been hunting for years as a cell mate to try to get the information needed for another trial. Mike could care less what his cell mate's name was other that what he was told by him. The first day he set eyes on him he had told Mike his name was Dutch, Mike replied by saying his name and they hadn't had that much to talk about since. Dutch was easy to live with and only one time when he had tried some of the drugs in the system did he ever talk about himself. He had been convicted of murder with a life sentence for shooting up a gambling room apartment when he caught them cheating. The funny thing to him was they were all friends, had gambled together and drank together before many times and he was sure they had never cheated him before as he seemed to always be ahead or about even after a game. When he realized what was going on, he pulled out his lucky little twenty two caliber pistol he should have left at home, but had brought it along to show his friends, now enraged and drunk, demanded his money back. All four had been drinking and they just laughed at him with his cute little gun which infuriated him even more and he started shooting. His close friend died first and the rest thought it was an act between them and kept laughing and telling the friend to get up and stop playing games. They woke up to the truth when he shot the next one and the blood from the big neck vein showered the table with blood as he died. The other two broke for the door and he just flung a shot toward them as he sat down exhausted. He was still setting there with his little pistol in his hand when what seemed the whole police department came to get him. Dutch didn't give them any trouble and at his trial, he made a deal to escape the death penalty. He accepted a life without parole judgment and had been inside nine years. He was a good candidate for the nut ward from what Mike could tell. Once, Mike would hear him defending himself to another prisoner by saying it was all self—defense, and if they didn't have guns, they should have bought some. Although Mike tried to ignore what was going on about all the publicity about him being an innocent man in prison, but when one popular lawyer told the press he was on the case of justice for the innocent, he agreed to meet with the attorney to talk about the crime he had been convicted of. He knew almost nothing about the case himself, because he was drunk at the time it supposedly happened and in the trial he had been stupid enough to let his so called attorney handle everything. The brilliant lawyer told him he had to review what the judge and prosecution had before he even came to see Mike. After several months of what the lawyer called negotiations between himself, and the courts, and with numerous newspaper stories across the state about the lawyer talking about the honor of helping Mike, seen on television almost every night, he was advised to accept the court offer by the lawyer. First he had to plead guilty to second class murder, and the conviction of first degree murder would be thrown out, and he would be sentenced to twenty to forty years in prison with time already served counted against the twenty to forty. This meant a possible parole in just over eighteen years. He really thought it over seriously because he was the type of man that felt if he had done wrong, he had to pay with time in the prison system and when he was released he would know what? Maybe that he had served twenty years of his life for something he hadn't done or that he had beaten the system and served only twenty years for a double murder. He prayed over it and asked other inmates about it but everyone had reasons for doing the one thing rather than the other. He was shocked to find out the lawyer that had been helping him was now about to be appointed by the governor of the state to the empty seat on the state supreme court, and didn't have enough time to talk to him. Mike immediately realized that he had been used to get the judgeship and then found out that if he would have signed the paper to second degree murder he would then have to bargain with the state to close the deal, as it had never been approved by any government panel, and the governor who would have to sign off on it hadn't even been told about it. The hurting part was when he found out that if he had signed the paper, all appeals would be terminated, he could serve the whole forty years with no reason for parole. By signing it and turning it over to the warden, he was admitting guilt which he had never done before, even if they turned it down as a deal, he knew or suspected that a copy of it would be in his records with the GUILTY word in it. Mike told them no deal and appealed to the same state supreme court for help in getting a new trial. He was now ninety nine percent sure he had not committed the crime of murder on the two people. Newspapers across the country picked up on the duplicity of the lawyer using the inmate as a way to get publicity so he could get the seat on the court, but it was too late for the governor to back out now and the attorney's name was submitted to the state senate for approval as the replacement judge. Local groups across the country started drives to; FREE MIKE; and other prominent lawyers tried to contact him to offer their services, but now he was gun shy. Mike now had served twenty months in prison and was sick enough of that terrible smell that he now was thinking of what many men thought of in prison, suicide. It began to enter his mind more now and he had even started to collect information on it from fellow prisoners, such as what worked faster, least painful and silently. He seemed to have something a little more than other prisoners thinking about suicide because he truly didn't know if he was guilty of the crime that had been committed. Life goes on though and Mike didn't consider himself the only wrongly convicted prisoner in this prison and others who thought they had been treated unfairly began to contact the people trying to free Mike. It wasn't unusual for fifty or more prisoners to want to join the big movement starting up in this state and others to help people who felt they had wrongly been convicted of crimes. It was on the television and the radio talk shows and it seemed that every person in the country had a personal view and wanted to share it. Political action groups were up and running about the subject, some demanding this and others were demanding that. Honest groups were pushing on it and dishonest groups were feeding on it with phony ex-prisoners telling of the misery of serving time when they were wrongly convicted only later to be found out by newsmen with integrity that they had never been to a prison, even as a visitor, and had been hired by the networks to perform. One so called former prisoner could not describe the prison he spent five years in supposedly as an innocent man. He had been given a list of things to study before being brought forward to expose the system, the only thing wrong was he couldn't read and lived on the street ignoring the list. This went on all summer and then a strange thing happened, people started demanding answers to the problems from the leaders of the country and even stranger, the political people got involved. Many people were invited to testify before congress including Mike but this caused a problem with the state. Who would be responsible for those prisoners when they spoke before congress? Of course the congress said the states would be responsible, to which the states, who were actually working together for once, replied the prisoners would then appear before congress in the familiar prison uniform of white with black stripes, with the little almost sailor looking hat, leg irons, and handcuffs. The prisons wanted the congress to guarantee the return of the prisoners, pay for their transportation and security rather than send guards and equipment to the capitol, all at cost to the states, and they didn't want to spend money they didn't have. The truth being that most prisons didn't even use the black and white uniforms anymore and didn't have any, but the congress didn't seem to know that. Now no congressman wanted to be seen on television grilling a helpless man in white and black uniforms with leg irons and handcuffs, but the states had the feds by the short hairs and wouldn't give in. Congress then asked three very old Ph.D. recipients to testify about the subject and they talked for three hours a piece, drank copious amounts of juice and water and said nothing that anyone understood and after spitting in their hankies all afternoon left the hearing room with wet trouser pockets and everybody was happy and closed their hearings. Meanwhile back in the prison Mike and others went to work as usual and Mike marked his second year in prison. Nothing had changed that much over the two years he had been there except the feeling of hopelessness was gnawing a little harder on him and other prisoners for different reasons. Obsessions always seemed darker when they were woke up in the middle of the night by a screaming prisoner, who may have been having a rough dream or he might be being raped by some animal that used to be a man. He might just be getting sliced up like a piece of fruit because of something he said or did somewhere sometime against one of the crazies. They had also caught one nut screaming in the night just to frighten all the prisoners. The craziness never got better or worse but drifted into the medium of both. It seemed like every day; someone he knew or had heard of either died, was murdered or sent to the cooler. He sometimes likened it to a large tornado dark storm cloud on the horizon and coming fast, swallowing up everything in front of it as it, chewing it up and spitting it out behind as it closed in on him. He was losing his memory of people and places on the other side of that giant wall. He no longer cared what others thought of what he said, thought or did. Hope was almost gone. The time came when it was considered desirable for the people of the world to stop whipping on each other and help the downtrodden, or at least that was the message of the political party out of power trying to get back in power. There was too much pampering of convicts and prisons should be tightened down to reflect the American ideals of doing the time for the crime without all this fuss about if someone was guilty or not after they had their day in court. The hopefully incoming party said if elected they would open every case of misjudgment of a person in court if after a hearing it was found to be flawed in any way, the person given a new trial. Then if found guilty a second time, that prisoner would then serve every day of his sentence, no matter what. So in November the voters picked the other party to take over the government and not a thing changed, no tax change, no responsibility movement at all and the often mentioned prison reform movement slowed to a crawl. This has been happening now for over two hundred years and people still believe it or say they do, until the next time. It has been a tradition in the state government to propose changing something just to please a certain group or section of people and get there votes. When they found out the other side was more numerous against it, they wined it wasn't their fault. The California law, Three strikes is a good example, but they forgot to build prisons to hold all the three time losers. Every day seemed like a week and Mike now had thirty months in prison and had lost so much weight that he looked different than the somewhat softer looking two hundred thirty pounds. He now looked the part for one of those old prison movies where brutality was the main feature and escape was the only way out. The young face was now lined with new creases and his weight was down to one hundred eighty pounds. It wasn't that he looks so skinny, because he still worked out and his body showed the results with what looked like solid mussels covering his body, but his eyes showed defiance to most things about the prison. His attitude was completely changed about almost everything. Even his parents had stopped visiting him in the prison because of his attitude and his very apparent use of scurrility when he talked of prison life. They didn't give up hope, but they weren't going to sit through that again. He was falling into the same quicksand most lifetime prisoners do and he was close to becoming what he disliked so much in the prison. He remembered back about twenty two months ago when they had first brought up the idea of maybe getting a new trial, he hadn't believed them then and was glad he hadn't. He found reason to quarrel with anyone when he was down, which was most of the time. He reminded any person talking to him that he was an innocent man in prison and it was obvious that he was truly losing his grip on sanity. Although by now he had probably forgotten it, he first came to hear that a prisoner was innocent on the first day in prison from the first prisoner he had talked to. It seemed to be a disease that was caught by everyone at some time, depending on how long you had been on the inside. The head guard kept a highly secret journal know only to the other guards supposedly, but leaked to the warden years ago, just what prisoners were reaching that stage of their confinement that the guards had to watch closer than the others because sometimes they flew into a rage and killed some other prisoner or themselves. Mike's name had been penciled in recently and was under a close watch. Unknown to him, his shop was checked every night to search for any evidence that he was planning a suicide or something else, like maybe a killing or escape. Nothing was ever found but the checkers did notice that the machines once again needed cleaning and oiling, just like before when Charlie was going downhill. It wasn't as if they ran around the prison hunting for something to do, they had plenty of their other duties, and babysitting any prisoner was onerous to them. They knew it might sound like extra work for them, but getting the prison back under control after some nut ran around stabbing other prisoners would be extra work too, as would anything like this big guy going off the beam and stirring up all or most of the other inmates. Then one morning, The black clouds lifted and the world changed as he was suddenly called to the captain's office in the early morning and told to pack his stuff up and be ready to roll the next day at eight in the morning. "Don't leave anything because I don't think we will be seeing you again". He knew better by now not to ask where are we going, or how do we get there? So, that was how it was going to work out he thought. Unknown to him was the fact that some individuals with nothing to do with the prison system had been working on a new trial for the past three years and had finely convinced the right individuals to agree. He had not been told of the badgering that was going on in other places about his punishment, indeed his whole trial, and it came to fruition only in the last two weeks. He wasn't to be told he had been granted a new trial while he was in prison. He had reached enough maturity in this prison to know there would be no answer to any question regarding his departure. Just be ready to go at eight with all your possessions. That was all he was told but it perked him up enough to tell others he was leaving as he went around to different acquaintances to say a hurried goodbye, which was answered as always by not much more than a wave and a grunt. Those staying had seen it before, and would again until someday they might be the one leaving. He had no idea what was going on, for all he knew he was going to another prison or maybe he was going to be taken out on the street and sent on his way. He was changed enough to have wanted someone to say thanks for the work in the machine shop, but it wasn't forthcoming. He wanted to set down with someone in the system and tell them what they were doing wrong and what they were doing right. For a moment it even seemed ludicrous even to him to think the people who ran a prison would like to have a critique by one of their prisoners who was leaving on undefined terms. He reminded himself to get serious about this new adventure or he might crack up. After he had turned in his key to the shop for the last time, he was told to report to the property room and pick up all his possessions for tomorrow. He took the smelly old box to his cell and waited for morning. It became apparent the next morning after sleeping little that night that nothing much had changed, he was in his own old suit but a new set of leg irons and handcuffs on and he was warned that he was not to talk unless asked a question. Here he was, being driven out the gate he had come to believe would never open for him again. It was pretty heady stuff, but he was up to it. He was finely told where they were headed for. It was about a two hour drive to the court house where he had been sentenced, so it was pleasant to see the other people and cars on the road. He thought it hilarious that here he was, probably on the way to some kind of hearing to find out if someone else would give him a chance to prove something he had no knowledge of. He didn't feel that relieved about the whole thing because he wasn't told enough to get his hopes up. Contrary to what was supposed to happen, he was not told that he had been granted a new trial. Later he would think of it as the last rebuke from the warden for getting a second chance at life. He was guarded by one guard sitting up in front with the driver with automatic locked doors in the rear, and a thick wire screen between the front and back seats, with the guard snoozing most of the trip. The back windows were inoperative so it was quite stuffy in the car. The driver was a trusty who was afraid to talk to him and would prove to be a terrible driver, so everything was cool. He felt like a deep sea diver coming up from the bottom of the ocean, sometimes he could almost see the sunlight on the water and other times nothing but darkness. Out of this darkness would come all sorts of vicious looking sharks with the faces of some of the prisoners he had known in the past three years. He knew he could not get too anxious about reaching the surface or he would fail. Fail at what, he had no idea. He wanted so much to push his face up, and feel the sun on his face. Mike was lost in thought and for some unknown reason was thinking about his younger sister who it seemed was so shocked at his trial that she never came to see it. She was a real beauty even then at seventeen and they had a special thing between them that she always checked with him before starting something different, including boyfriends. She had never cornered their father as she had him to ask some pretty touchy questions about things the parents would never consider proper talk between either of them and her. Their father would have preferred she went to a doctor to answer her questions, but she had tried Mike as a last resort and he had no problem answering her questions. From then on, she never worried about something she didn't understand, she just asked Mike. She had never said a word to him about the circumstances surrounding the murders; in fact he hadn't seen her since being arrested. If he ever got out of prison he had no plans to make it any harder on her than he had already and would wait for her to come to him if she wished to talk. He knew his parents were hurt badly by the whole mess, but he hoped he could make it up to them once he was freed, if ever. He was drowsy and thinking about his freedom and was having one hell of an organizing performance going in his head as if he was on his way to someplace unknown. First he playfully played the game what if with himself. What if he could get the leg irons and handcuffs off, get the doors open on the car and run alongside the car in the fresh air, not to escape, but for fresh air or what if they got into a traffic accident and he couldn't get out of the locked backseat, and burning up in fire, and all the firemen were sitting or standing around a large table playing cards watching him but not trying to help, and if no one showed up in court and he had to stay in the back seat forever, which he didn't care too much if they brought him lunch once in a while. Just don't bring any more chicken sandwiches. The crazy thoughts came and went. As far as everything went though, if he got out of prison even for a short time, he was planning on a nice week or so to himself with no one around to think about the past three years, plan on his future, change clothes from that stinking prison smell that had crept in the suit while stored in the smelly prison, and eat a good steak. He seemed to know he was dreaming as he worried about someone waking him up because he knew he was smiling. Mike was off and running in his day dreams and eventual light sleep. There he was pulling on a soft good smelling white shirt, and a great looking suit coat and stepping outside his house with no restraints. The day was beautiful, the sun was shining and a beautiful Kathy was standing with his parents, brother and sister, obviously waiting for him, everyone talked low and smelled so nice; when a loud close car horn noisily brought him back to reality. He woke up quickly and cautioned himself about planning the future when he was hardly free and might not be for many years. He knew something was up concerning his future residence but not what. It was not a big thing when he recognized the court building where he had been sentenced. Here he was again, same time, same suit of clothes, only three years difference. There were not too many people around the court house as it was probably lunch time as his stomach reminded him. They parked the car under the courthouse and the driver stayed with it. Mike thought it funny that here was the driver in a car with the chance to flee as soon as they were out of sight but would be there waiting for them no matter how long they were gone. A prisoner known to Mike as Hootie, and he had no idea where he got that nickname, serving fourteen years, with seven already served, for a drunk driving accident that killed two high school kids and the driver of the vehicle, while riding with a much wanted man driving a stolen car. They had been out scaring the daylights out of small store owners, showing guns and taking everything they wanted. Along the way they began to drink some of what they had taken from a liquor store and lost it all. Hootie's friend didn't make it out of surgery so the judge doubled up on Hootie. The guard took shuffling Mike in the back way and up to the sixth floor to a small courtroom. They didn't say a word to each other, but he noticed the guard check his pocket and looking at some instructions on where to go and how. They had a seat without asking anyone and immediately jumped to their feet when the judge came in and asked the guard to remove the hand cuffs and leg irons, so here he was standing there with none of the prison hardware on, feeling almost free and still wondering what was next. There were only two other people in the court room, no spectators and the lady with the machine she always seems to be typing into. He noticed she had beautiful legs. The judge was not the same one who had sentenced him to life in prison. He had prepared himself for that guy and was relieved it wasn't he. This one had a nice smile on his face and didn't seem to be in a hurry like most judges. He asked Mike if he thought he had received a fair trial three years ago and he said no, the judge then asked him if he wanted a new trial, this time shaking his head no as he said no. He then asked what he wanted and Mike quietly told him he wanted his freedom because he was innocent of the crime he had spent three years fighting. "I'm afraid I can't go that far "said the judge, "The best I can do is a new trial, even if you don't want it. That is the rule of the courts and I guess you know that a new trial is better than to have to go back to prison." The sudden quietness in the large court room begged for somebody to say something and Mike answered with the pretty sharp "I will take the new trial your honor". "Ok young man, this court has now granted you a new trial as ordered by the state, bail is set at two million" said the judge "and your new trial can be scheduled for two months from today in this court room if you agree, or later if you have council that thanks that is too short a time. " The smiling judge continued on looking straight at Mike. "That is fine with me your honor" the weak voice of Mike sounded, cursing himself for being too easy to agree to another trial. He didn't know why he was so mad at everything, here he was with a new trial, another chance to be free and his attitude was about to make things difficult for him. He was taken to the holding jail below the court room where he was signed over from the prison legally, ignoring the offered hand shake by the prison guard and already thinking about the bail he couldn't afford, no way would he agree to that same lawyer he had in the first trial. He smiled for the first time in a long while and thought about some of those characters in the prison who were jail house lawyers who could do better than the lawyer he had in his first trial. He felt good not walking in those leg irons and handcuffs and with just a slight touch of a guard on his lower back guiding him where to his surprise his family was waiting for him. They had been notified by a friend they had made in the court when they were still trying to get a good lawyer for the first trial. He had called them about the appearance of Mike the day before him and had almost guaranteed his father what the bail would be. Without asking him they had already hired a well-known attorney and arranged for bail. Mike had no idea what the cost of all this was, but he would find out and repay those who had helped. He felt that he had let everyone down before, and wasn't really that sure he wasn't just dreaming. His mother ran forward to hug him and then the whole family surrounded him ignoring the guard who promptly tipped his hat and left. Inside his mother's mind after looking at her first child's face was a cry as she looked into vacant looking eyes and the stern face of an almost unrecognizable son. The whole family was there, his look alike brother and his sister Marcia, mother and father, and the attorney Gordon Plenty. He didn't look as big as his reputation but had some very sincere looking eyes. He was about five foot ten and one hundred sixty pounds it looked to Mike and he liked him right off for some reason. They shook hands when his father introduced them and Mike felt good for the first time in months. Attorney Plenty was as true in life as he had heard inside. His reputation was about as sincere as one could be and the respect other prosecutors and attorneys had for him was tremendous. One of the constant jokes in prison had been about Attorney Plenty. Two prisoners would be talking about how they were railroaded to prison, and another prisoner walking by would say "Should have had Plenty". He was well known in this environment by many prisoners, some having been on the receiving end of his renowned ability when he had made a good case for pleading guilty and not facing the death penalty. There were numerous stories about him, some untrue, but most very true. The most famous story about him was when he was asked by the court to defend a man accused of killing a cop. During the trial, which he fought like he was getting double his regular fee, a rookie guard in the courtroom was about to take the prisoner to lunch in the basement lockup when he somehow got hold of the guards pistol and held the whole court captive for an hour by grabbing Mister Plenty and threatened to kill him if anyone tried to stop him. The attorney kept telling him to put down the gun before someone got hurt, but naturally he wasn't listing to anybody. The people in the audience were all pushed against the far wall by fear. The jury ran out of the jury box and through the judge's chambers followed by the judge. The crazed man mumbling threats against everyone and sticking the pistol sometimes into the back of Plenty's head and neck leading the attorney out of the courtroom and down a hallway with the uncocked gun to his head and an arm around the attorney's neck heading for the elevators they guessed. He was quite tall but very skinny and stood above the lawyer. Now; here is this large hallway with about twenty policemen with their pistols out backing down the highly waxed floor, and another ten or so officers behind the attorney and escaping felon, as it appeared to be a struggle for the criminal to make up his mind the way to go. When the very unafraid looking lawyer asked one more time for the killer to stop and reconsider what he was about to do, and when he just grunted, and didn't answer, Plenty suddenly stopped walking, rammed his right elbow into the man's stomach, reached over his head grabbing the killer by the hair and ears, throwing him over his shoulders, and on to the floor breaking his arm as the lawyer grabbed and held on to his gun hand. Well that was the end of that court day as cops swarmed over the killer. What was even crazier was the fact that when he was repaired six months later and ready for another trial, Plenty defended him again and had to question himself on the stand as he was a witness to the escape attempt but his luck ran out when his client was found guilty and sentenced to death for the murder of the cop. He had tried to tell him to make a deal to avoid the death penalty, but he was all through with this life and told Plenty he didn't want to live in his world anymore. When his time came to die, several years later, Plenty was asked by the prisoner to be a witness at his execution and watched him smile his way to the other side of life. This helped steep the reputation of this average size man into almost fanatic belief in his power over juries. This same attorney now in a much better situation said he would be at Mike's house that evening at six for a long talk with him, but right now he should celebrate with his family for a while. He drove off in a beautiful expensive car. Mike and his sister jumped in Cecil's truck and headed for the family home about three hours away. Marcia was quiet for the first ten minutes then squeezed his arm and started talking and never stopped for the next three hours. She was never so alive in her life and explained every action she had taken in the last three years on every subject, person or thing. Cecil was not used to hearing these kinds of talks between his sister and brother and was almost embarrassed at some of it. He knew they had a close relationship and was proud of them for it. Mike said very little, just enough to encourage her to let it all hang out but he was happy she still loved him enough to ask for guidance from him. Poor Cecil couldn't get a word in edgewise, and just listened to the fantastic calmness in his brother's voice when he would caution her about something or say it was a great idea. Mike sat there thinking about what his sister was asking because he felt she deserved his attention and the time flew by so fast he had no time to think about that foul place he had lived in for three years. When they finally pulled into the driveway of his father's home, he was feeling like he needed some sunshine. He endured three hours of talking to his parents, brother and sister in their parents' home, all of them having numerous questions about prison life, eating some good cake and a cold glass of milk, before easing outside where his brother gave him his keys, showed him where he had parked his car when he had retrieved it from the impound, assured him it was now in good running condition, gave him a strong manly hug and went inside. Mike went to the home he owned and lived in the same area about two miles away. Waiting in his driveway was the lawyer who had just arrived and the two sat in the living room for the next four hours discussing his case. First the attorney informed Mike that he had been a friend of the dead lawyer and knew him very well, in fact he had warned Caldwell to stay out of those little bars at night because he could get robbed or roughed up. Mike was dumfounded that this lawyer would agree to defend him when it was his friend that was the victim. The attorney could see the puzzle on his face and explained that number one, he thought him innocent and number two, everybody needing a lawyer should be able to hire anyone, no matter what, if he thought himself wronged, even by a relative of the victim. "Now, let's get to work" said the lawyer. What time did he go to the bar? Who was with him? Had he had a drink any place other than Toney's? The questions seem to never stop, and as he answered each one, it was recorded on the small recording machine that the lawyer had brought. It became apparent that this man hired by his father thought of Mike as an honest and straight forward man entirely innocent of the crime of murder and intended to prove it in court. As he was leaving Mike's house, Mister Plenty asked him where his car had been the night of the murder or had he walked to the bar." I parked it across the street from the bar and it was towed the next day while I was in jail" Mike told him. "My brother got it several days later and took it home, why do you ask?" "Just thinking", said the lawyer as he left the house. It was nice to be home but the place smelled almost as bad as the prison and he couldn't live with that smell again. Although his brother had done a tremendous job starting everything up again in the house, he hadn't had a chance to have it cleaned yet. If someone had come to see this big man cleaning the house, they might think he was trying to wash the paint off everything. He looked to be laboring at something he hated and was trying to do away with. He had taken off all his clothes and put on an old pair of shorts and started cleaning. He vacuumed and scrubbed, and if it didn't smell right, he vacuumed and scrubbed again. The suit he had worn the first trial and had lain in that prison storage soaking up all that terrible smells, he put in a plastic bag, tied the top securely and threw it in the garbage can, not wanting to contaminate his can with that smell from the prison. For the next four hours into the wee hours of the morning, he washed and scrubbed all his loose things in the house, washed all his clothes, the floor, and the curtains. He wore himself out with the cleaning and almost fell asleep in the shower where he wrung every ounce of hot water from the tank as he scrubbed himself as hard as he had the possessions in his house and fell asleep on clean fresh sheets straight from the dryer. He was too tired to dream but once during the darkness of early morning he was awakened by what sounded like someone in his back yard. He was too tired to even check on it and was soon sound asleep again. He was pleasantly surprised when he opened the front door about nine am and found several quarts of milk and a box of his favorite cereal with a note from his sister to enjoy his freedom now because later she was coming back for some advice about her life. He was in a great mood as he had his cereal, the first in three years. There was cereal or what they called cereal in the prison but it had the same smell as everything in there and he could not eat it. As he cleaned up the kitchen and took the little bit of trash out where he thought he saw footprints in the dirt outside the kitchen window but wasn't overly concerned as probably over the last three years homeless people had noticed that his house was empty and used the parts of it they could for shelter even if they couldn't get inside. Mike was just thankful that they hadn't been living inside all the time he was in prison. He did make a quick inspection of the lock on the gate and realized that he should get a replacement for it. He was stunned when he jerked on it, it opened without the key. He kicked himself mentally about the lock, remembering it was very old, and had been on the gate when he bought the house just about a year before this whole fiasco had started. It might have been the noise he had heard last night, people who opened the lock when checking on him. Then too, it might have been the gas and electric company restoring power as his brother had requested when he found out that dad was going for the bail for Mike. He made a fresh pot of coffee in anticipation of the promised visit from his sister, read his newspaper that his thoughtful brother had started again and was relaxing on the couch when she arrived with a big smile. They spent the next two hours sharing stories of how their life had evolved in the recent three years. She had a bold question right off the bat and as he thought of how to answer her serious question, he noticed that she was very much a beautiful catch for some lucky man. Her question had been about the homosexual problem in prison; basically what she was boldly asking was, had he participated in any of this kind of behavior, had he been raped as she had heard of these things happening in prison? When his almost choked laughing stopped, he told her the real story of the homosexual in such a place and no, he was still a virgin with those guys. She seemed to have changed little while he was in prison, maybe more pretty, but she still suffered from trusting him to guide her in her life, and he felt funny knowing that anything he advised her on became part of her life. She was in love with at least four guys at the same time, had not been intimate with any of them and she wanted Mike to pick the best from the pictures she had. He was very careful with that job and begged off on making a choice for her. He thought to himself; sure I tell her who is best and he turns out to be a snake in the grass, who was going to catch hell from everyone? It didn't bother him in the least that she talked in such personal terms. Just like if he introduced her to Marcel as he knew he wanted him to do, his parents wouldn't approve of anybody that drank with him, and he would have to fight them for something he didn't want to do anyway. It was decidedly lonely when she had to leave but any difference of their beliefs in the past three years was laid to rest. That was when he decided to introduce his attorney to his sister as soon as he could, as he had heard about his first wife. His sister was very frivolous in most things, and Plenty was serious in everything, so maybe they could help each other. In the next several weeks he had many visits from his family as if they were afraid he would be taken from them. He tried to get one hour of sunshine every day, and like the prison he wasn't happy when there wasn't any sun. He made sure that everybody had a key to get in the house when he was outside in his chair in the afternoon sun. If not you might have to stand out there for a very long time waiting for him to answer the door. He also had many more visits from his lawyer who he was beginning to really like and as he was an old bachelor, he delighted in introducing him properly to his unmarried sister and they took to each other very fast. Mike didn't think the thirty years difference in their ages would matter at all. Just by the way they kept looking at each other all the time they were there was amazing to Mike. He could almost feel the sparks between them when passing through the room. He was so happy for his sister; he wanted to yell out loud. They had been on several dates already and when she started talking about his lovely house, he could almost hear wedding bells. He knew his sister and he respected her privacy so he didn't pry into the obvious love affair between them, and knowingly she didn't discuss it with him. Hooray for her, maybe, just maybe the intimate side of her would not be part of their discussions anymore. It was time for her to lean on Plenty from now on. It wasn't that he dreaded the upcoming trial; he just didn't have time to worry over it as his confidence in his lawyer climbed higher and higher. There was time for thinking and sunshine and trying to clean all those memories of the three years in prison from his mind so in between working with his attorney every day, trying to help his sister who had a thousand questions a day, most of them now about Plenty and his plans and needs and getting plenty of sun, he stayed busy. He had taken to drinking some vodka most of the time and it seemed to be part of his day whether he needed it or not. He had borrowed two thousand from his mother without his father's knowledge and it was going pretty fast so he had to warn himself to slow down. He loved setting out in the sun with a cool drink and just letting his mind wander, and also hoping that his memory of that night would slip in unnoticed. He was not so lucky at getting his memory back as he was getting a terrific sun tan. He was still considered to be guilty by his old girlfriend Kathy he guessed as she had not called to say hello or welcome home, he realized that if and when he was found not guilty by a jury the calls would return. It didn't bother him that much, he hadn't heard from Marcel or Bud either. In some ways it was truly strange as some of his old friends received subpoenas for the second trial yet had not called to say hello or acknowledged he was now at home. It bothered Mike more than he liked to say about no one calling or coming around to see him and he asked his brother Cecil what he thought about it. Cecil told him straight out that he wouldn't visit someone who had just got a new trial after putting up with prison for three years. Mike was amazed and asked why. Cecil told him straight out that just because he had a new trial did not mean he was innocent, after all, twelve jurors in the past had thought him guilty enough to send him to prison, and now twelve jurors had to find him innocent enough to set free. It just meant the court didn't like the way he was convicted. He smiled and told Mike "We are not talking about family here". He at one time after being bailed out thought about going to Toney's maybe to have a couple drinks. Just maybe the whole nasty dream would wash over him and he would be free. To know what? That he was a killer? That one of his friends had done it? No thanks, he did not want and was afraid of getting close to that place, besides he had heard that business was way off since the murders and they weren't open every day. Sometimes during that two months he could almost feel the memory coming back, in fact one day when it seemed about to reenter his brain, he tried very hard to reach out to it, and it was instantly gone. Next time he made up his mind to not try to force it to come back, but help it by letting everything in his mind go blank. That was very encouraging as he did for a flash of a second get some results, but to him it meant nothing for all it was, he saw himself sitting on a bench sleeping on an almost but not quite known street at night. As soon as he pushed on it to show more, it was gone. He never tried to guess what happened that night because he didn't trust himself to be honest with what he might see. The two months went by very fast, Mike looked decent and huge and had even grown a beard, but his lawyer told him that juries didn't like beards, and without any questions, he quickly cut it off. He was tanned and well—dressed most of the time and the trial was now set for the next Monday, with all the witness he could think of and many doctors were subpoenaed and visited to confirm his beliefs and his lawyer that it was impossible to kill in the condition he was in that night. He was also convinced that wondering if he was guilty or not only muddled the brain and ordered to wash that thought from his brain. He met with his family once more before the trial and he even had a large smile on that occasion, the first and only one in front of his parents since being arrested almost three and a half years ago. It was a cool and windy morning on Monday when the trial opened and it was mostly dull legal stuff about picking the jury which wasn't dull to his attorney. Plenty knew what he wanted in a juror and if someone was very close to being what he wanted, he would question him or her until he was sure that the last part was there, He cared little for the idea of race or religion or age as a challenge to that person as a juror. Sure, if someone who looked perfect and was educated good said something bad about what his client believed in, worked at, or lack of patience about the case, he would be dismissed straight away, and if he had an old man, black, white or Jewish who had what he was hunting for he would fight to keep him. He placed a little sized woman named Junie with a snappy retort to each of his questions on the jury, hoping she talked to the other jurors like she had talked to him. He made no secret to his staff that he hoped she would be chosen as the foreman. Attorney Plenty was the type of lawyer that didn't take short cuts with jurors, and he preferred that they convince him of their impartial beliefs. Listening to him question a prospective juror was sometimes like sitting in a cooking class at some university because when he had a women to question, he would often go deep inside her to talk about cooking just to relax her. With a man it might be fishing or woodworking, you name it, all just to make the jury relax and feel at home in their trial. He always made it clear that this was their trial, their job, not the Judge's, not the prosecutor, and certainly not his responsibility. He encouraged them to think; We instead of I. He told all of them that what he wanted was a clear verdict based on what he and his staff and yes what the prosecutor said with no doubts. If they couldn't work under those conditions, he requested they quit now before he proved to the world that his client was innocent of the crimes. He didn't allow clients to take short cuts with his stated price for representing them in a court of law. He never publicly told anyone what he charged and never would come down one inch from his stated price. He didn't charge the same every time and he sometimes worked for free if asked by the court. He felt duty bound to get the very best jurors even if they had to panel a new bunch and postpone the trial for months on end. He picked one man without final approval and stayed with him until he could get somebody with just a little bit more of something he wanted in a juror. He felt no obligation to the man and when he found a housewife with that little something the man didn't have, he quickly dumped him for her. He refused to even question one women who had a monster of an admitted hangover from the party she had gone to in celebration of being on the jury panel for selection. When the jury was picked after two days of haggling and using up all his challenges he was satisfied with the jury of seven men and five women. He never second guessed his choices and if they voted guilty for his client, he knew he had screwed up in picking the jurors. The four alternates he treated the same way as the other twelve, hard facts only and "We have all the time in the world", was his saying. That he would feel it was his screw up picking the wrong jurors may sound hard to do but Plenty always believed the prosecution did the same thing when selecting jurors. He had used a little influence in the prosecutor selected for the retrial. He quietly asserted his clients rights to a fair trial and when they tried to give the case to the same nasty one as before, he promised fireworks and a grand jury investigation before the trial was one day old. They juggled their lineup and said the prosecutor would be Edward Macey but that Plenty would be sorry because he was a real hard dude. Plenty knew Macey and respected him. They weren't friends, or enemies either but both would great each other when they passed in a courthouse or trial. Macy was married with three girls, all teen agers and he suspected that made him harder to beat in court, by Plenty's thinking, how a man could live with four women in the house and not go crazy, or as thick skinned especially three teenage daughters, as to ward off all challenges to anything. As too the jury selection and when asked by a junior lawyer why he did it this way, he replied "Is there another way?" It had taken some people a long time in court against Plenty to realize he never stopped working for his client, not at lunch, not on Sunday or not even when he was enjoying himself with Marcia. All this preparatory work took time, in fact up until about two in the afternoon of the third day, when the opening statements were introduced, first the prosecution then the defense. The case against Mike was tightened up somewhat in the retrial, and they still insisted he knowingly killed the older couple in a fit of blind rage when intoxicated and when refused a session in bed from the beautiful older half-drunk women. Her blood had revealed a high level of alcohol at her autopsy as had her husband. It was their belief that he thought he was being picked up by the older couple and when refused sex, he battered and choked both of them to death, losing his jacket in the fight with the two, as they fought the much younger man. He then tried to flee from the scene but was spotted by the bus driver and arrested. The defense now had their turn and It was much different than in the first trial with attorney Plenty contemptuous of the made up case of the prosecution to accuse this honorable man who had served his country in Vietnam with honors, and with an almost unseen flip of his hand, one of the junior attorneys approached the jury and passed the certificate he had been given by the helicopter crew in Vietnam for being aboard when hit by enemy fire. Mister plenty talked for the next fifteen minutes about Vietnam and never mentioned the case they were working on. He must have mentioned the word stress a hundred times and only when he noticed the judge beginning to blink off did he start on the extremes of alcohol and promised that many doctors would testify as to what alcohol does to the body. He ended his one hour summation with the chilling words "While you have this sham trial, he may be hunting for his next victim, maybe your family". There was only time for one witness after the opening statement and that was the chief investigator the night of the murder. He was a hurried looking man, but competent looking and he had been in the job for many years, had a mixed reputation as he had been involved in some questionable behavior. He was a large overweight man with quite a stomach, gray hair in spots and thick glasses at sixty one, and close to retirement. It was obvious that Macey knew how to get down to the bare facts when he had the chief even testifying to the condition of the street where the murder took place. He was known to be a rather emotional person who was afraid it seemed to talk about his past too much. He was a married man with no children and no one seemed to remember what his wife looked like. He was rarely seen with his wife at public places, and had no children that anyone knew of. He testified to all the pertinent information already known by everyone and seemed bored, sort of like in a hurry to go someplace. He had a rock solid opinion that the defendant was guilty as charged, Macey guided him through the whole investigation smoothly and efficiently and Plenty knew that most of the jurors were now thinking that Mike was guilty as charged. He testified for a solid hour about why he thought Mike guilty, and most of it was very plausible. Now as it was time to cross exam, the judge wondered if the defense could wait until tomorrow to do it as it was rather late in the day to start something he guessed would take quite a bit of time. This was part of attorney Plenty's strategy and when the prosecution had first called their first witness, he had sent two operatives out to verify all the facts surrounding a case of child neglect somehow involved with a Mister Oncody, the chief investigator several years ago. There wasn't a scandal brewing about it, but it might come in handy in getting the judge to ok an end of the day if Plenty could plead that the two investigators weren't back yet and he needed this evidence to prove the defendant not guilty. There seemed to have been some cover-up suspected in this case and others with this witness. Plenty was literally licking his chops at the thought of the cross exam of this person and wanted no night off between the start and finish of his time. He had no intent on a cross exam of Mister Oncody today even though he knew he was taking a chance with the jury allowed to leave the courtroom, some thinking his client guilty, but he had some magic for tomorrow maybe. If need be he would fake a heart attack to get the judge to wait until tomorrow for the cross exam of this witness. A secret out of town trip after a midnight phone call from a woman he had never met, or knew of where he had spent a couple hours listening to her very angry and confused story and believed it would swing people's minds in the jury tomorrow. It was obvious from what she said that not only did she know what she was talking about, she had solid proof of what she said, with pictures. She refused to give the lawyer any of the proof to take with him and demanded and gave instructions on how to use what she had given him. She did admit to hating Mister Oncody but not why other than what she had shown him. Plenty had been waiting for the judge's request, to stop now and continue it in the morning. "Fine with me your honor" Plenty answered the judge and court was dismissed until tomorrow. Mike was tired and glad when the first day was over and when he was tapped on the shoulder just before standing up, he was surprised to see his attorney in the first trial, Mister Render. He apologized again for the lousy work he had done in the first trial and wanted to talk to attorney Plenty about something, and he felt it proper to go through him first. Mike introduced them and left the court house with his family. After the trial was over Plenty told Mike that Render had turned in his resignation to the Bar association and was going into being a friend of the court, which helps poor people charged with a crime among other things. He held no grudge against him now; it was too late to undo all the damage he had done to the beliefs of Mike. At one terrible point in the three years he had been locked up, he had prayed that he would see him again just so he could beat the hell out of him, but now he knew it was an empty thought and he just wanted to forget his name and face. When he was home alone again, he pulled out a fresh bottle of Vodka and had a strong drink before doing anything else. Mike was seriously considering calling his old girl friend when the phone rang. Not knowing who it might be, he took his bottle with him to the couch by the telephone. "This is Mike" he said "How are you holding up Mike?" said the familiar sexy voice of his former girlfriend Kathy. He relaxed all over and sat there on the couch talking to Kathy for the next two hours about everything he could imagine to keep her on the line, but he didn't have to work hard, she said she was still his girl if he wanted. They had always had an easy time talking to each other, ever since the day he was working as a lifeguard at the beach and saw someone floundering in the surf and had quickly gone to her aid. They had first became friends, then lovers but not so serious as to prevent him from going in the Marines when she went off to college. She was now a very qualified tax lawyer with several degrees who made good money at saving people money on their taxes but needed help just like everybody else did with regular lawyer problems. Try as she might, she couldn't explain to friends and relatives why she was hanging around with a common laborer, now prisoner, when she could have her pick of professional men she associated with daily. Now it seemed to be one more chance to go forward in life together. She was close to being considered an old maid by some. They quickly worked out a plan for him to stay over at her house as soon as the trial was over. "Hey, I might be found guilty again" he shouted and she returned with the comment that his jail cell bed better be big enough for two as she hung up. He was in a super mood as he prepared for bed with a strong pull on his bottle about ten o'clock in the evening, and again he was awakened in the middle of the night by sounds outside his bedroom window. He considered the noise outside almost provocative, like someone was making the unnecessary loud noises to draw him outside where he could be killed or wounded. Perhaps if he had never participated in a war or been in the Corps, he might have accepted the challenge, burst through the window and bellowed "let's get it on". This time he called the police like normal people and they responded quickly and found footprints in the dirt below the window. They promised they would look around the neighbourhood for any strangers but guessed it was just some homeless guy like he had thought earlier. As they were leaving, one of the cops recognized him and asked if he was the guy on trial, and when he said yes, the cop yelled good luck as he left the yard, probably waking up all the neighbors. He thought it strange that he had picked up the habit of going to bed early from being in prison where it wasn't unusual but didn't pick up other habits like smoking and dope. Mike was displeased with himself for sitting here at the table having another strong drink before trying the bed once again. He was beginning to worry he had a problem with booze, but he brushed it off with the reminder that as a man on trial for his life, he had the right to calm himself down when the pressure got too strong. He was concerned that there might be someone watching his movements and looking in his windows at night now, but it didn't seem serious enough to worry about. As he sat there he tried to think of whom it could be, that was harassing him. He wasn't worried as long as it was not threatening his safety. Sometimes he liked to think it was one of his distant girlfriends checking on why he hadn't called her as soon as the much talked about new trial hit the front page, but laughed at that side of himself for being too greedy. He had a pleasant dream about Kathy that night. He also forgot again to get a new lock for the gate. The next day in court was a very good day for the defense because Plenty acted like a general moving things here and there, canceling some witnesses, and calling for new ones to come later and always seemed to know what they would say on the telephone before they would say it. Then he had the job of cross examination of the chief law enforcement officer at the scene of the murder and it looked like a daunting task, but not to the attorney who seemed to have a different kind of smug smile on his face from the first question on. He first asked how long he had been an investigator and that was the end of mister nice guy Plenty. For the next three hours he tore the poor man apart with questions about his record as an investigator, and in the process ripped his reputation apart as a straight shooter. As fast as he answered a question, he was asked another, if he hesitated too long, Plenty would hit him with another and expects two answers at the same time. What about this and what happened there? Is it true that he badgered a suspect so much that he attempted to kill himself a couple years ago? Why is it that my client was arrested for murdering that lovely couple and accused of running away when his car was parked across the street? How do you run away and leave the means of escape behind? Once during the cross examination, after waiting for an answer, he strolled over to Mike, leaned down to whisper in his ear and asked him what ring size his sister wore, smiled when Mike tried to talk back to him, then calmly walked back to the investigator and shouted at him to answer the question. He was constantly like an actor on stage and some things, like the coming over to Mike was just show for the jury. Another time, he asked the judge to excuse him for a minute, pointed a finger at a man in the audience, motioned for him to follow him outside the courtroom, and everyone in the room heard him say to the lawyer "I don't care, I tell you I saw him" and just as quickly the door opened, the man moved back to his seat, and the lawyer profusely apologized to the judge for taking so much of the court's time. He started in again on the investigator. He promised that he would have many witnesses testify as to the lack of honesty on his part from past cases. Which one do you want me to start with? Is it true that you have been locked up in your own jail for crimes against the public?. Plenty unrolled an official looking paper, looked at it, then asked the witness "I see from your discharge papers from the US Navy that you served a very short time, could you tell us why?" asked Plenty. It seemed to most people; what was he doing with the discharge papers of another man, wasn't that illegal? It seemed the whole world was waiting for an answer to the question. A slight cough in the back of the room got a stern look from the judge, and the buzzing fluorescent lights were about to get chewed out it seemed when the judge looked sharply at them. "I don't know why" he finely answered. "Do you want me to refresh your memory sir?" "No, I was released because of a bad mistake" the investigator said. "The bad mistake being what?" Plenty shouted. "Some liar said I was taking drugs" the blood red face of the chief said. Plenty looked shocked and recited the kid saying." Liar, liar, pants on fire." Plenty held the empty sheet of paper up in his hand and smiled, and came back with many more questions. He gave him sufficient time to answer but most of his questions weren't meant for him, but for the jury by innuendo. Just when it looked as if he had destroyed him, the attorney seemed to think hard for a long second, start to ask a question then stop and think about something very deeply then he asked him one more question. "Do you know a Sally Rully by any chance"? The investigator choked, jumped to his feet and shouted/ begged out loud "Please, not that." "No more questions your honor" said Plenty very quickly as he took his seat. The witness was now again sitting in the witness box with his head hanging down as if he was waiting and dreading the next horrible question, or waiting to die. The man who had gone outside the courtroom with the lawyer got up and quietly left the courtroom. The judge was asking the prosecutor if he had any redirect for the witness and when he heard no, he asked the broken looking investigator to step down. As he left the court room he looked at no one but his appearance had changed remarkably to that of a haggard swollen eyed determined man on the way to fix something and seemed to be in a hurry for some reason. Several minutes later after regaining his equilibrium from the court room, he hurried to an empty elevator and almost closing the door, even as other people were trying to catch it. While they stood there cursing the man, there came a loud explosion from the elevator. People standing there jumped and tried to run as the roar seemed to follow them, there was a total panic, especially for those that had never heard a gunshot that close before. It was heard all the way into the courtroom and stopping all action at once. All of the police personal in the courtroom drew weapons and rushed for the door to check out the obvious sound of a gunshot. The first police to get to the elevator had a bazar sight as a buzzing elevator with intermitting bells ringing and lights flashing as a human arm lay stretched out from inside the elevator blocking the door from closing, and thus stopping the elevator from working. It took just a second for the officer to hold the door, then push it open and push Stop on the panel. There on the floor lay the chief inspector, almost unrecognizable as part of his head was blown away, leaving a terrible mess of his face and the elevator wall. The police took charge immediately and cleared the people from the area and calling for emergency help. The rest of the court day was suspended when the judge reported to the court that the chief investigator for the county and recent witness at the trial now in progress had just committed suicide in one of the elevators in the courthouse. The shock of those words first rang through the courthouse, then every other place in town. Everyone was asked to leave the whole area of the tragedy in the building and the investigation of the suicide of their own boss began by the whole team of investigators. There was disbelief from many of the city staff, no one could remember this ever happening before in the history in this county and the coroner who was a cousin of the investigator locked himself in his office and wouldn't come out until he was assured that his cousin had really killed himself and not somebody trying to kill off the family one at a time. To be sure, there were some people who decried the way the attorney had publically caused this terrible thing to happen. One news headline saying there was no time for this kind of legal brain battering causing such a terrible killing and the lawyer should be barred from the courts. The trial was delayed for the rest of that day and another day plus the weekend while an investigation was underway. The newspapers were full of stories about the investigator, both good and bad.

There were many stories about the life of attorney Plenty too, bringing stinging memories to him about the murder of his wife and the rumors about how he had executed the kid on the spot for killing his wife. Some people even got to see the investigators wife for the first time, when she was caught by an enterprising young reporter following a hearse leaving the hospital and nothing else to do, called in the license plate number of a car she was dropped off by and it was quickly traced to the inspector's wife. He followed her from a distance until she stopped at a medical drug store and waiting for her when she came out. He took several up close pictures of this decidedly determined looking women without her knowing it and rushed them back to the newspaper. They were the headline news of the paper the next morning after their agents checked the pictures from her driver's license with their own just to make sure it was the right women. Her phone had to be disconnected because of the calls, and she went into hiding to prevent more pictures of her in the press. She was a young lady, looking to be about thirty, about half her dead husband's age when he killed himself. She was well dressed and pretty, and a disappearing master. The press treated her like she was the one behind Sally Rully, or maybe having been Sally Rully before she married the chief investigator. When she even refused to come out of hiding to clarify the mystery, the press printed half—truth stories other so called news magazines had written about her. The investigation into the suicide of the chief investigator ran straight into a brick wall. Attorney Plenty was questioned several times about the way he performed his cross examination but it was all legal and above board and as was his right he refused to divulge who this person ; Sally Rully was, even to his client. The investigator's friends were questioned, as was their wives, even the judge was asked for his comments, all to no avail. No one could find the man who had talked to Plenty outside the courtroom, and the attorney wouldn't identify him and refused to say if the short talk with the missing man had anything to do with the suicide. Close associates of Plenty were told over a later time that the whole thing was a sham to get the investigator more shook up and it had cost him two hundred dollars to hire the gentleman from an ad agency. Meanwhile Mike enjoyed his three days off with his brother and sister. His sister had recently moved into a new apartment close to where she worked as assistant editor of a neighborhood newspaper when she wasn't in school at the university. She was doing very good at the paper that had started as a free weekly into a heavily advertised weekly that made good money for the three that ran it. Of course the smart brother was just about to get his Ph.D. and Mike sometimes had to ask him to slow down when he was explaining something he had asked him. He had encouraged his younger brother to mix more with the sister, so they would all share the closeness that he shared with her now. The trial took on a whole new face as everybody in the courtroom was watching attorney Plenty more than the witness. They seemed to be waiting for more bomb shells. When the trial continued, there was much information from the doctor hired by the city to determine the cause of death which in layman's terms was strangulation; the victims were in good health generally and when the doctor was asked what would be his guess of time remaining in their life, he replied at least twenty years but it was a very hard thing to predict. Attorney Plenty didn't cross exam any of the doctors because he agreed with what they were saying and his experts sitting in the courtroom gave him the no signal. Even though the courtroom was packed and still abuzz about Mister Plenty, the day was very drawn out and everyone was relieved when it was over. Old time court watchers had never experienced a court week like it in several years. There seemed to be little sympathy for the now deceased chief investigator and a lot more good press coverage for Mike. Of course every news organization in the country was looking for the mysterious Sally Rully. There were many people, law organizations and even the local chapter of mad mothers and fathers against drunk drivers who claimed that the real Sally Rully was a child run down in the street by the investigator but offered no proof. They offered no facts about the alleged crime, and later admitted that one of their staff had misspoken. There were lines of people, mostly newsmen waiting to get certain copies of certain documents authored by the Chief investigator at the city clerk's office and almost brawling among themselves while waiting for this one or that one. Phone customers with any name close to Rully were being plagued by nosy people, lawyers and law enforcement people from all over the state. Attorney Plenty turned down magnificent sums of money and trips to fabulous places to divulge the story of Rully, but he just told everyone the same thing, he had pledged never to reveal the circumstances she played in the chief investigator's life. Even when talking with close family people, he would not mention the name Rully. He told close confidants that he had been prohibited from going any further than the name and the question had to be asked that way, should the investigator have answered the question in court the attorney had promised to stop questioning him immediately and excuse him as a witness. He was certainly not to tell anyone anything else in normal conversation. Even before this action, Mister Plenty had been known as a strong advocate of secrecy among himself and his clients so his friends knew he would never give up the secret, even to them. Back in court, after testifying that the man staggering down the street was ; sort of like the defendant, the bus driver Glen who discovered the bodies retreated under the hard cross of attorney Plenty and admitted that he couldn't identify the man or women who was staggering down the street. Plenty got him to admit it could have been a woman he saw. Plenty mentioned his glasses he had on and acted real chummy with the bus driver and how hard it was to take a whole bus load of people somewhere and bring them back after they had all been drinking for the past the past three hours or so. He was commensurate with the bus driver about how that would make him nervous, might even change what he thought he saw. The bartender also retreated from where he told the prosecutor he had overheard the defendant arguing with someone from the end of the bar. He admitted that at the time there were about twenty customers in the place and it could have been someone else. The bartender was also unable to ascertain how much money the defendant had spent during the evening after testifying to the prosecutor that he had spent a large amount of money that night. Plenty asked him why everyone should believe his account of how the bar was closed and he locked the door behind them." How is it that your DNA is found on my clients jacket", are you sure you didn't just step out after Mike had left his coat in the bar, choke the two for their money and throw the jacket in the alley but had to run back inside before you could get it when you heard the bus coming to a stop?" The crowd gasped, the jury gasped, and the bartender, being accustomed to being treated a lot better than he was now, fired back at this question and most of his answer was lost in the noise from the spectators in the courtroom. Most of the questions were accusatory in nature without directly accusing him and made strictly for the jury's ears. Firing back at each denial from him, Plenty asked him again how the DNA got on the coat. He finely admitted that he and others were admiring the jacket while Mike was in the bathroom and all had tried it on, so maybe that was the answer. "Not likely mister" roared Plenty. " What would Benbe think about that excuse" he continued. There were only several people in the courtroom who knew what or who he was talking about, and the bartender left the stand stunned and shook up that the lawyer knew Benbe but he had never seen him in the place. Plenty had no reason to believe Paul was the person that killed the couple because when he first talked to Paul while still checking on people before the trial, his people had told Paul that if he had ever been in trouble elsewhere, best to tell attorney now rather than face it in court. He had paid a visit to the attorney's office and told him about his time in prison for throwing the rail guard off the train. That didn't mean he hadn't killed the old couple, but it never entered their conversation while he was on the stand. Half way through the next day, the prosecution announced it was finished with the case and the defense had their turn. All of the friends from the first trial testified as they had in the first trial, and with a great bit of shaking her enormous weight around like a big bowl of jelly, Benbe testified for the first time. It was another bone head maneuver from the first trial lawyer that she was of no use to them in the first trial. Now Benbe testified that in girl talk in the bathroom with Mrs. Cambell, she said if they ever had a chance they would want Mike to be a big brother to their children because he was so mature and even though the same age as their oldest son they realized from meeting him several times in Toney's place that he was very mature and could teach her children a lot. "Have you ever seen anyone trying my clients sport coat on"? Plenty asked "I did once but it was way to small" she giggled. Under cross examination Macey tried to shame the witness by asking her how she could say such things about some one's kids after the murder of their mother. She answered very sweetly that she was just answering his question. He tried to paint her as a drunk that hung around with other drunks, but she had everybody in the courtroom laughing, including the jury when she gave her analysts of one who drinks too much and started laughing and each roll of her body started rolling. Everyone in the courtroom was laughing, the jury, the judge and the prosecutor. He gave up and even gave her a hand getting down from her chair. One would think the case was moving right along. Then there was a stir in the room as a uniformed policeman was called to the stand to testify that on the day after the murder he did ticket a car parked on the street across from Tony's bar because it had been parked in the zone to long. A check mark on the tire said he had been parked for at least eight hours before a tow truck was called and the car was impounded at 11:45 am. "Did the officer know whose car it was?" Yes", the cop said, and opened his little ticket book and said "it was registered to Mr. Mike Williams". Everyone in the court room expected something big was up, but the cop was then dismissed without any cross exam, but you could tell from the prosecution table that they were surprised by the witness and what it meant. Very soon after the policemen left the courtroom one of the prosecution team went rushing out of the courtroom. Later talking to a friend Plenty admitted that testimony from the cop had been brought in just to confuse the prosecution as to where Plenty was going. This was something planned over a period of time, with a subpoena being served during the officer's duty time to make sure he came in uniform. Then the different kinds of doctors started parading to the stand telling all they knew or thought about drinking inordinate amounts of any alcoholic drink and what effects it had on the body and mind. For the next three days it seemed that every witness called to the stand was a doctor, had been a doctor or was going to be a doctor. It was so boring that Plenty said later that he seriously thought about just sitting down and waiting for them to start talking, sort of a turn on switch, and later get up from his seat and turn off the switch. It was quite frankly very boring to most of the people, but just what the Defense Attorney wanted. He constantly watched his jury as to their attention, and when the right ones started nodding off, he would finish with the witness and call another boring one. He was gambling with twenty five years of experience and it was working. It was a lot of hard work, but he ate it up. He had the jury so confused about what the truth was about what doctors knew or didn't know about alcohol that they were ready to be handled with kid gloves and told the truth, from who; ? Plenty of course. What studies were being done in different countries, how important it was to remember the facts about what they were testifying about and what it meant for future generations. It was all very interesting but only if you had attended many hours in school on that subject, or been a bartender for about thirty years. Although pleading innocent to the charge from his friends after the trial was over, it was believed Plenty brought all these doctors and Ph.D.'s to show to the jury how confused the world was about what alcohol does or don't do to the brain when drinking large amounts at one setting. He realized that every professional, be he doctor or research specialist wanted to get their word in on their beliefs on what it all meant. He hoped that most jurors would try to remember all that junk, and then when it was impossible, forget it all and realize all people, regardless of many factors of race, height, and ages were affected by alcohol differently. Then he called the family doctor which didn't turn out too well it appeared at first, when he testified that Mike seemed to have a low tolerance for understanding others and losing control of his emotions and temper when in a prone position and after arising too fast from the near prone position. Under cross examination the doctor said it was noticeable in test after test and would not be dissuaded by anyone and also under cross exam when asked why, he mentioned flying in a loud plane at low altitudes and he had noticed it in Mike when he returned from the Marine Corps." Was it dangerous?" asked the prosecution. "Not unless you were getting beat around the head and shoulders, and fell down during the assault" answered the doctor." Would it be affected if this person were drinking heavily? "The prosecutor quickly asked. " Depending on how much drink was taken, the effect would double every few minutes", answered the worried looking doctor thinking about losing Mike's family appointments. Plenty didn't seem concerned and asked the doctor on redirect how many people in the country were suffers of this condition and the doctor said very meekly "about two thirds. "Plenty then dismissed him and called his next witness which was the doctor on duty at the police station when Mike had been brought there. This Doctor was a man so convinced that he was going down in history as one of the greatest, and was very proud of his physical fitness that he wore clothes that made sure you saw him as a master at physical fitness. His ego was almost as big as Plenty's and he was all of twenty seven years old. To himself Plenty was saying "God is that what I acted like when I was that age?" He had no idea what the Doctor that this man worked for wanted when he found out he would be called as a witness. All he had said was if you have time during your questioning of him, he wanted a favor. He just told Plenty "I want you to trim his sails some". After the usual questions about his qualifications, time he had served as a doctor and how long had he been on duty when seeing this arrestee, the hardnosed defense attorney casually asked the doctor what the readings on the different methods and gauges were when Mike was tested for drunkenness. "Oh he was too drunk to test after being brought in so they confined him and let him sleep." the doctor gushed. "I don't understand Doctor, you say you have been a doctor for one whole year, a medical doctor working at the city jail for three months and already you have acquired the ability to declare a person drunk without a test of any kind, the medical schools must be fantastic dwellings now days or you are an excellent doctor far advanced of the average doctor," Plenty yelled. He was still trying to explain himself when Plenty yelled at him " no further questions Doctor" making the word doctor sound dirty. Mission accomplished. Sails trimmed smartly. Now, the attorney was well aware of what the policies were when bringing in a drunk for any reason when he was out cold, the same as had happened to Mike, but the public didn't know that and Plenty wanted to give the young man some help in his study of court procedure. The prosecutor quickly said "no questions your honor". The judge then announced the day's business was completed and rose to leave the room. As he stood there he caught the eye of Plenty and with a slight movement of his head invited him to the judge's chamber. When Plenty reached his quarters, the judge had already shorn his robe and was mixing two drinks of bourbon and water when he yelled come in to Plenty's knock on the door. The judge pushed a drink across the desk to Plenty and said "Gordy I don't want any more suicides in this trial so take it easier on your witness when you ask those brutal questions." Plenty laughed at his friend John and said he was getting ready to slow down in this case anyway as he felt victory was close by, but he knew he had been chastised to take it easier on witness from his old friend. They enjoyed several drinks and talked about their annual fishing vacation coming up soon before Plenty left the chambers. He had no intension of going easy on any witness but he would restrain his voice level to make it harder for the judge to be concerned. John realized that having a drink with Plenty was ok, but as the judge, he could not have a drink with the defense attorney. Mike understood how the system worked and John had once been a partner with him until he tired of always being the devil in a case, using hard words and tricks to get what he wanted out of a witness and instead became a judge and lord of the court. He had been a very good attorney and made a lot of money which he delighted in watching his wife spend. When they were young and he was just getting started, there wasn't too much money around so his wife worked as a salesclerk in a clothing store for women, bringing home just enough to tide them over until the next case he could get as a lawyer. When they started doing well, he insisted that she stop working and start shopping. He was rated as a good judge and fair to all sides, and she was known in the circles she traveled in as the best dressed women in the place. Her husband swelled with pride when she headed out the door dressed so well, either with him or alone. If anyone who knew either the Judge or the attorney or both, and that person claimed the Judge helped the attorney in court, many other people who knew them both would be very upset. There were times in the past when during a trial with John on the bench and Plenty serving as attorney that cross but legal words would fly between them when one or the other thought the other had overstepped the bounds of their duties. Most times in those cases, when the final verdict was in, you could find them sitting in the judge's chamber having a couple drinks together talking about fishing. Plenty sometimes wondered if he should quit lawyering and retire like John although he was coming up on only his twenty fifth year of his career, with his fifty first birthday coming up pretty soon. His bank account seemed to overflow some times and he had to hire a professional money manager to keep it straight. Even before her death, he couldn't manage money very good and neither could his wife. She was ten years younger than him when they got together and she kept herself and him in shape by sometimes getting on him when he made excuses to miss working out by parading by him in very revealing clothing and making some excuse when he wanted her to come to his bed. His wife had been and was in his mind, a lady of extremes in almost everything concerning their marriage and they were extremely happy together whether working out together or in the bedroom or traveling around the world. He considered himself an extremely lucky person to have the life he had. They had a serious talk before they married and both of them were happily surprised that neither of them wanted children, both wanting to adopt young teenagers when they had succeeded in their own right. Then the world caved in on him when his wife was killed during a home invasion robbery at their winter home in California. Some little vermin looking young man had invaded the house through the side door he had left unlocked for the expected return of some of the housekeepers out having a day off. Plenty was upstairs in the shower when he heard his wife scream just as he was exiting the shower. He ran to what she liked to call the setting room where he thought she was, just as he entered the room, he was stunned by a blow to the head. He went down hard but never lost consciousness and guessed that it was better to pretend to be unconscious for the moment, even though he expected his life to end with a pistol shot to the head. He was also stunned to remember what his mother used to call him when he was a kid; rock head. From the floor, after a couple of minutes, he could see his wife just a few feet away lying on the floor, eyes wide open and looking dead. He watched as the skinny housebreaker went from drawer after drawer very carefully and slowly, sometimes smelling her fresh underwear, apparently thinking he had knocked out or killed the attorney when he hit him in the head. Although he was hurting quite a bit, and bleeding from the head, he remembered the pistol he kept under the sitting room couch, just inches from where he had fallen. He slowly groped for the gun, hoping the little thug hadn't found it. His little finger touched something cold and steel and he had to fight back the urge to grab at it, stand up and start shooting. He knew he must take it easy because the eyes were still a little slow to focus after the blow on the head. Slowly he tightened his hand around the caliber thirty eight pistol with six slugs in the round chambers. He opened the pistol with professional skill not needing to look at it and felt all six bullets in the chambers; he didn't have to check what kind of ammo he had loaded in the gun, because he always kept flat nosed bullets in this pistol. Closed it carefully, silently and slowly brought the pistol out planning on shooting the thug before he knew it. He thought of his wife laying there in a pool of her own blood with a bloody doily lying near her, where he figured the killer had wiped the blade clean after killing his wife, and decided that to shoot the worm with no warning was too good for him and opted be the vengeful person he now felt like. Plenty quietly cocked the hammer back set up suddenly and said "Hey pimple face, over here". When the young pimply faced youth turned quickly at the sound of the voice, surprised to face Plenty sitting on the floor, naked and wet from the shower, blood dripping from his head he almost turned green when he saw the pistol. He started to plead for his life from what he could see in the attorney's eyes, and the front of his pants suddenly became wet as his fear caused him to urinate on himself. The first shot from Plenty was very intentional and tore off the right ear of the little killer and spun him around so he was bent over and facing away from Plenty holding his ear and screaming, trying to hold his hand over the wound to stop the bleeding and the pain. Plenty got to his feet, the room still ringing from the shot, his head still ringing from the hit on the head, staggered a little, checked his wife for breath and finding none, reached over to the young man still screaming, spun him around yelling " look at me pimples". When he did manage to make him stand upright, he looked terrible as his ear, or where his ear used to be, was bleeding profusely and his right side of his body from head to toe was red with blood. He was crying like a two year old, as the attorney then backhanded the youth with the pistol, the front site opening a cannel across his cheek, nose and other cheek. His scream of new pain was drowned out when Plenty then shot him once in the groin and once in the head as he fell to the floor, only after the ringing noise of the pistol died away did he call 911. That his wife had been stabbed repeatedly and the knife was in the dead man's knife scabbard on his belt was obvious. The police were in no mood to question the shooting in any way, as Plenty had all the required papers and license and he was well respected. There were no questions about the number or placement of the shots and they didn't even ask him about the closeness of the shots. In all probability some of the police to answer the 911 call didn't believe all the gunshots were necessary, but they kept it to themselves. It was believed that one of the detectives later fired for testifying untruly about a comrade's conduct in a police review case, wrote a book about the shooting and called it an illegal execution. When asked about it by a news organization, Plenty neither denied it or admitted to it and told the news he was sorry about the author losing his job with the police for lying under oath and that if he believed his own story, he should take to his old comrades. The dead youth was identified as a suspect in other break-ins and was well known to the courts. The twit was hauled away, probably to end up in a pauper's grave, as his parents had cast him aside some time back. Attorney Plenty had a very tough time, and more than once brought out the same pistol to use on himself, put it up to his head and took the slack off the trigger but every time got stronger and put it away, still he almost didn't make it through the year ahead. At no time did he even call his office or try to contact the many clerks and junior lawyers, but they read about him in the papers once in a while when he was still recognizable to the public. If he hadn't been fortunate enough to be very wealthy and smart enough to hire the best people to work for him at home and office, he would have just faded away and died. The payroll officer kept everybody working by paying the usual salaries from the very hefty banking account, and the chief of staff kept their old and new clients happy. It was fortunate that he had no active cases at that time because he was only thinking about his grief and had no time for anyone's legal problems. His domestic staff came to work regularly, cleaned the house if he was home or not, generally acting the same way as always. They had the sitting room repaired from the bullet holes in the walls that had torn large holes in the intended victim before tearing smaller holes in the walls and furniture. Wherever they found him asleep or passed out, they worked around him and got that place the next time when he was passed out somewhere else. Most of the time, his house looked like a train wreck or as one gardener suggested, it looked like one of those old bar room fights in the movies had gone on in his house when they came to work, so they knew he was having a terrible time trying to survive. He would go from whiskey to wrecking in his misery and no one wanted to interfere. They just kept repairing what damage they could and trashing that which couldn't be repaired. His money manager made sure everyone was paid, and life went on. Sometimes he could almost be recognized when he shaved or took a bath, but mostly even those that knew him had no reason to see him unless they went slumming in the bars he now drank in. He was at one time arrested for sleeping on the street and thrown in the drunk tank, unrecognized the whole time except by the desk sergeant who passed him through the system unknown and no holds, released the next morning. He went on monumental month long drunks and tried to hurt everyone the same as he had been hurt, he stood in the darkened bedroom waving the pistol around and cussed out God with the same fierceness he would again use against unsuspecting witness someday. For some good reason, he never took his pistol with him even when he tired of cussing out God, he always put it away before heading into another night of trying to forget somebody he had loved more than anything in his life. Slowly he regained his sanity, and one day he shaved, showered and came back to work. He looked terrible, he had lost at least forty pounds so he looked terrible even in his hand made suits, said good morning to his staff and went to his large office. His junior partners and office staff had known from friends of Plenty that he might be coming back to work and when he was seen by one of the office staff getting a haircut at his favorite shop, they were sure he was coming back. When he did come in, he was treated as if he had never left; no one asked him how he felt, or where he had been for nine months. It was just as if he had gone home the night before and returned this morning. He was the same man, but he wasn't as mellow as he had been and somehow he seemed to be a bigger man than before. Things that irritated him before were now accepted and his manner of conversing with his junior lawyers now was filled with concern for them more than the business. He was like a kinder, older man, but his eyes still showed the misery of losing his beloved wife. Some of his close friends were very concerned about him and some worried about how he seemed to delight in grinding a suspected liar on the witness stand after her death, like he was blaming the witness, but at the same time it finished the making up of this one tough attorney. He was relentless when questioning, even when questioning his own witness if he thought they were not trying to remember what they knew. No person ever questioned his effectiveness though. "That is one hard dude" said a hard suspected little mafia witness leaving the stand after being questioned for one hour by the attorney, and copied down by one of his aids and presented to Plenty on a beautiful Mahogany wooden sign about thirty inches long. It was still hanging there today. Mr. Plenty in tender moments with Marcie admitted that sometimes he did lose control when questioning a person just like Mike's doctor said he lost control when he got up to fast, but that was what an attorney was supposed to do, to a point. By the time Mike and his troubles were laid before him, he had recovered about ninety percent from his ordeal of running from himself. The next day of the present trial would be the big test as he had decided to put Mike on the stand to testify on his own behalf. Actually he hoped to put the right words in the young man's mouth because he knew he remembered almost nothing from that night. He had never asked if he was guilty and didn't think it was needed now. When he had first started being a lawyer, he sometimes worried about helping out a criminal but he also believed in himself and the system and never asked a client if he was guilty. He preferred that the subject wanting his help to be innocent but if the client confessed to him he was guilty, he would still work very hard to get him the best sentence by plea-bargaining, but would not otherwise take the case even if offered tremendous amounts of money. All of this was explained either by one of his staff or by Plenty himself. His way was to assume that all his clients were not guilty and all of the other procedures were to prove it to a jury he had a strong hand in picking. Mike went home that night trying to control his nervous brain thinking about what would happen tomorrow. He was a little angry at himself as he suddenly found himself sitting in the living room watching himself on television in court today, with a glass of almost pure Vodka in his hand. He had a hard time falling asleep but forced himself to stay in bed when he heard movement outside his window. There was no fear as much as self-disgust for himself for not remembering to get a new lock for the gate. He listened very carefully and just as he decided to speak out to the person outside his window, the glass, curtains, and window frame were destroyed by a huge cement block, from his patio he found out later, followed by a fire ball of flame flying through the window. He leaped from the bed just as the fire caught his blanket and seemed to eat it up like a frenzied cat. The fire came from a huge towel tied on the end of long stick also from his patio, but soaked in gasoline before lighting. The noise, light and smell were terrific and his first instinct was to get out now and almost ran from the house, but instead beat down the flames doing the most damage as the training in the Marine Corps jumped in his heart and he ignored a small burn on his shoulder and continued to beat out the flames enough to call 911 for help. The good people in the fire department quickly got there and only used their small hoses to put out the fire because he had been quick to beat it back when it came through the window, but he wasn't about to get any more sleep in that bed for a while because of its wetness. The police were outside checking for clues and they wanted to talk to him about this incident and other reports they had from him about someone harassing him at his home. This fire thing wasn't considered harassing though, the police had much stronger words for it so when they sat down to talk to him, they passed knowing looks at each other when he told them about the trial, and that the couple he was accused of killing had two grown sons who had voiced hatred of him in the first trial. After they left, it was too late to go back to bed and he had called his dad to explain what had taken place. In minutes the whole family was there except his sister, in his damaged house trying to baby him. He finely decided to go to his parents' home until the damaged items were replaced and the water and fire damage repaired. The only thing he took from his house was the clothes he would need that day in court and his half bottle of vodka. His mother gave him a choice of his old room before he moved out or one of the others, but he felt better in his old room which still had some of the fixtures it had when he had left for the Marines. It was still early in the morning and he decided to have a drink and get some sleep. He was trying to get away from the flaming ball of fire, but wasn't doing too good a job at it and he was getting nicked up with tiny burns every time he looked at the fire ball. Then he figured it out; there was a man on the other end of the ball of fire and he seemed determined to stick it his Mike's face. He had to see the face before he could stop the fire, but every time he got close enough to see the face it was a different one. Then he felt the shaking and he seemed to be floating finally waking up with his father shaking his shoulder. The dream went away with his father who couldn't seem to leave the room fast enough after waking him up at seven thirty for court. While in the room, he noticed the almost empty bottle of vodka Mike had forgot to put away when he lay down. His father being a one drink straight shooter, and sort of snob, gave him a disapproving look, but said nothing to him about his habits. Mike knew he had screwed up and tried to explain to his father, but he was also a little tired of being a mister nice guy all the time, and almost got off on his dad. Once again he bit his lip and remembered he was in his father's house by his invitation but he just couldn't get him to smile that big prideful smile he had grown used to. He promised to himself that his father would be smiling again after this trial. He believed in his own innocence to a point, but he suspected that his father had a more compelling view of the whole situation and believed him guilty. He thought to when he was eleven years old and had taken a bike that wasn't his and dumped it in a swampy area just to be malicious. Someone had seen him riding the bike and when the parents of the child who lost the bike heard that Mike had been seen writing it, they came over see his parents and ask questions. Mike remembered with dread how his father had asked him numerous times if it was true about him riding the bike, and every time he had said no. After the other parents had left, his father had praised him for standing up for himself against accusations of being a thief. For many years he had wanted to tell his dad the truth about it but could never get up the nerve to do it. "No "he answered what he knew was the first of many questions starting with; did you kill that couple? He realized that his lawyer was guiding his every answer and almost telling him what to answer, but suddenly he was bone tired and didn't care about what was being asked or what his answer was. Lucky for him his lawyer recognized it and expected it and planned it that way. It was almost like having a puppet doll in his hands and crafting every answer, every question, and every sigh. He remembered later thinking that the attorney must have hypnotized him and even after his denial, he wasn't sure. Now; he brought the real Mike forward, the kid who wanted to join the Marines, and the finished product. A man more eager for war, than the disgrace of the fear he found in his own heart. At one time he had him setting in a bunker in Vietnam with rockets crashing all around outside, just knowing that the cracking noise meant that it had hit a little too close and another had him visiting an orphanage where hundreds of Vietnamese children, some with no legs or arms were being cared for by the Marines in his company. Alarmed to find he did care for other people and the ability to help those little ones. Tears were plentiful from this grown man and real because he had reached a moment in his life where he had never been before, or if he had been there before, the Marine boot camp had taken it away, now believing that he was not guilty of any murder and feeling sorry for himself for being in this terrible mess. It was not hard to understand how this huge broad shouldered former Marine could appear so moved by remembering a war from eight years ago and no one there in that court room believed him to be faking it as plenty of the spectators dabbing their eyes. When Plenty at one time during the testimony turning around once to reach for something on his table, he noticed several women on the jury wiping their eyes. Now he bore down and asked questions he had prepared Mike for; like his opinion of the dead couple, which went into great detail about how strong they were and how they managed two major careers at the same time and raising two children. This continued on for two hours, having him give opinions of people involved in the case and in no way was he ever demeaning on anyone. Plenty said "Thank you Marine" before letting him down off the sky. One of the police guard in the courtroom when asked his opinion what had taken place in the court room that day said " I have been in the courtrooms in a lot of trials and before today I had never seen war veterans duck their heads and wince when a lawyer was bringing out the incoming rockets details of the defendant." Suddenly Into this roaring tangle of self-pity and tears, jumped this new voice, the prosecutor. It now was the main job of the prosecutor to show him up as a lying monster who used booze as an answer to fear. "I understand you served in the Marine Corps in Vietnam and were discharged as a sergeant, is that right Mike? Mike quickly caught a deep breath at being called Mike by the prosecutor and felt the fear crawl across his chest, slow as one of those nasty bugs in Vietnam. "'Yes sir" he answered and they were off and running on a two hour rampage through his fears, likes and dislikes about that country, war and prison. He got him to admit that he had been afraid when he had barely mentioned it even to anyone in the family. The prosecutor had many questions about the other prisoners in his prison, Were they mostly ex-Marine? Did they set around and talk about the difference in the killing in Vietnam and killing in this country? He was a master at insulting and he could tell that Mike was getting angry, exactly as he planned so he would flame up and say something his lawyer hadn't put in his brain. The prosecutor brought him through every course, with a slight sneer of disrespect to keep him boiling, he had taken in training on how to kill an enemy, with the whole emphasis on strangling being brought up front. Mike was asked to demonstrate a number of ways he was instructed on how to kill with a knife, but Plenty came out of his seat yelling at that and the judge instructed the prosecutor to stick to what was germane in this case. He insisted that Mike agree with him that it had all been a mistake and he had lost his head in an alcohol cloud. He didn't seem discouraged when Mike disagreed. He again told the prosecutor he had no memory of choking anyone. He asked Mike to show the jury how to strangle someone the Marine Corps way and as he talked he pushed almost physically against Mike just a little too much. Mike came out of his seat from the sitting position, way faster than the prosecutor thought possible, clasped the prosecutor by the shoulder, turning him around and against the railing in front of the witness chair very fast with his left arm around the neck of the middle aged man and tightened his grip just a little with the other arm holding his left arm against his throat. He gasped and some of his team quickly got to their feet, and Mike smiled and asked him if he were ok as he released him gently with a wide smile on his face. He was the only one with a smile on his face, because Plenty had jumped to his feet too; white faced and scared, later to say he only wanted to stop the prosecution team from interfering in the demonstration. He later admitted to one of his aids that he thought for sure their client had gone postal. There were no more questions that day or the next because they would give their closing summation after a day's rest. Mike went home with his parents and on the way his father looking in the rearview mirror and spotted Mike's eyes asked his son how close he came to choking the prosecutor when he demonstrated the choke hold in the courtroom today. Mike only answered as he always had to his parents, truthfully when he answered, "Not too close, just enough to frighten him." His father was shocked at this truth and wanted to ask more questions, but he didn't feel he could bear the answers. In fact he wanted to stop the car at a park or something like a park and take a long walk with him, sit on the grass, just talking, maybe about the Marine Corps as he knew his son really loved it, but here he was suspecting his son had somehow become a stranger, maybe it was too late anyway, if only he had been more observant before. He was unsure of what to do so he chose to do nothing. He knew Mike was trying to reassure him that nothing had changed, and as soon as this trouble was behind them, everything would be ok. After court that day he made sure he took time to get a new lock for his fence and on an off chance stopped by the DMV to see if he could make an appointment for a renewal on his license and was informed that he could take the test right then if he wanted and save the other time for something more important. In thirty minutes Mike was once more on the road with his business at the DMV taken care of. He felt edgy and as soon as he got home he had a good pull on the vodka bottle and tried to relax. He was sitting there trying not to think of anything, especially anything important when he had one of those elusive ten second day dreams. This one was him going to the bathroom at Toney's, probably the night of the murders as best he could remember how he was dressed that night. Try as he might, he could not extend the day dream even a second longer. Unhappy with life, overburdened with worry about his conduct when drunk, proceeded to get smashed again before going to bed. Mike and his brother spent the next day cleaning his house after it had been repaired and promised payment from his insurance company. They seemed to have forgotten that on the next day, he might be on his way to prison if his attorney's summation wasn't too good or the showboat prosecutor had a good day. It had dawned on him that as this was a separate trial from the first, not only could they find him guilty; they could even send him to his death. Mike wasn't worried about that but he was worried at what happened in court while demonstrating the choke hold to the prosecutor. When he came out of his witness chair, he purposely came up fast to test his former doctor's theory about losing control by getting up too fast. He had suddenly panicked when he lost control of himself and fought every inch of his brain not to snap the neck of the prosecutor whom he could feel was terrified. How about if he had a large drink of vodka before coming to court, would that have made a difference? Would two or three? He was once more unconvinced if he had acted the same against the couple. Once again his brain muddled by new facts that weren't clear and his strength taken away by something he desperately wanted to believe. Mike had thought about the facts of the murder quite a lot lately and wasn't afraid of the truth, but only because he believed in the way he had been brought up to believe in himself. He thought back to a time in Vietnam when he was driving a large truck, a six by, when he turned to miss a pot hole in the road and almost ran down a child in the middle of the road. He slammed on the breaks just before going onto the bridge across what he and his troops called the dirty water bridge. As he stopped, geysers of muddy water shot into the air as a strong blast of some kind of explosive floating on the water and shot at by a bridge guard went off scaring everyone on his truck, but more so his life as parts of the bridge railing disappeared up in the air and on top of his truck and others that has screeched to a stop when he did. The Marines guarding every bridge in Vietnam and it seemed this one had hit the jackpot and done his job when he had fired at the package floating down the river. Most of the time it was just a bag or box of garbage floating, but the VC had started putting small homemade bombs in containers and throwing them in the water hoping to kill someone, anyone dumb enough to be in this country it seemed. The bridge had not lost enough strength to be closed and after the Marine MP had screamed loud enough to be heard in the states, he drove across the bridge and gone on his way. He was shook up some, but it wasn't the first time he had watched a bridge guard shoot at something floating in one of the filthy rivers. Maybe if the little dirty kid hadn't caused him to stop, they would have been injured or dead. As one of his Marines said later, it was just another Vietnam memory in a dream someday. So, he wasn't new to sudden panics and when his brother broke out a bottle when they returned to Cecil's home and Mike almost refused it when in his head there appeared a newspaper headline saying ; BROTHER KILLS BROTHER WHILE HAVING A

DRINK! He wasn't shocked. He realized he had to get a hold on himself before he went batty. Meanwhile at the family home Mike and Cecil's father was thinking about all that had happened that day and he had a terrible day dream of his son Mike running down a street drunk and chasing two old people, a man and women, pushing a bicycle as they stumbled along but the Mike he saw was just a young man, maybe ten or eleven or so, gaining on them. Chasing after Mike was a judge in his long flowing robe, yelling something like; order in the court. Then some Marines, yelling something he didn't understand and then himself. He shook himself back to normal and his mind took him back to the day when his son had turned down the scholarship he had wanted him to take so much. Then his first son, his pride and joy had insisted that he and his mother listen to the Marine recruiter, after which he announced his desire to join the Marines. He thought to make his son happy by saying yes, but inside he felt betrayed. For a very long time he had to now admit, he had disliked his son intensely since that incident. He had found many excuses why he couldn't go to Mike's graduation from boot camp and sent his wife instead. He naturally thought he had worked so hard on raising his son that he would be responsive to his father's desires He had never told his son or anyone for that matter, that he had been rejected by the Marine recruiter when he tried to enlist during the very early days after the big war for his terrible teeth problem, later fixed by the Army when he was allowed to enlist. He didn't know himself if that was the reason he disliked his son and had to live with it himself. From the day Mike joined the Marines and on every day after, he worked on making Cecil what he had planned for Mike, an intelligent man of many strengths. He wasn't at all happy when this well-educated son of his started drinking with Mike when he came home from Vietnam. He was afraid for Cecil, it just didn't seem right to let the two set around and drink and enjoy themselves while there were things he had to be teaching Cecil. Sometimes he was afraid he might actually start hating his older son, but was afraid to admit it to himself. Mike had never done anyone in the family wrong; he was just strong willed like who? Me? It wasn't that he now really disliked his older son anymore, he just felt so disappointed and afraid he was going to lose this son too. When he talked it over with his wife, she very firmly recommended that he let the two boys have a little space to grow without his help, and stop trying to micro manage the lives of his sons. He got the message loud and clear from his wife and without a major interruption in their steady loving family life. Mike and Cecil had several drinks before he drove Mike home and helped him make the bed up before he left. He watched himself on the television until he was sick of the whole thing and was ready for a good night's sleep when the phone rang but went dead when he said hello, which happened two more times before he took it off the hook. This was getting to be a little annoying and he was starting to get his hackles up when from the front room he heard a very close gunshot, glass breaking and something falling in his front room just as another shot rang out and squealing tires. He became conscious that someone had driven by his house and fired several shots at his house, breaking probably a front window and something in the front room. As he hurried out the back door in just shorts, he heard the police siren go by his house chasing someone. In a matter of minutes they were back with a man in the back seat of their car. They were there to check on any possible injuries to him or were he hurt from the gun shots and mentioned they had caught the man doing the shooting. The one patrolman asked him, "By the way, do you know anyone named Grant Caldwell?" The memory card flashed in his mind and the Caldwell name got it. "Oh my God, that is the son of the people I am accused of murdering three years ago", moaned Mike. "Oh, so you are that guy huh, well look I hear you are going to have a big day in court tomorrow and we can't do anything tonight so we will book him tonight for attempted murder and the detectives will be out to see you tomorrow." After they left, he tried to calm his neighbors down, as there were about ten standing in front of his house, some angry at having such a notoriously loud neighbor, some wanting to help and finely he went inside sat down with a drink and wondered what the hell was going on in his life. Here he was, almost thirty years old, spent the last three years in prison for something he knew nothing about, some nut was running around shooting at his house or otherwise preying on him when he slept, he hadn't been out with a women for about four years and owed his parents about two years pay. It was now four o'clock in the morning and he was tired beyond belief. He had another quick drink and dove in the bed only to be awoken by the clock as soon as he fell asleep, or so he felt like, actually it was seven thirty in the morning and he was ready for court in no time. Plenty had a big smile on his face as they met in the court room, as he told Mike "Glad to see you alive this morning" without revealing how he knew about the attempted murder already. The prosecution went first and Mike was surprised to be called some names he had never heard before. He smiled to himself when he thought about his brother in the first row of seats with the rest of the family, thinking "I'll bet he knows what they mean". He was accused of every bad deed in the book by this actor/prosecutor with a neck brace showing brightly against a tieless white shirt to better show off his new trophy. He admitted to provoking Mike to show the jury that he was a monster, but he was not offended or sorry or thinking of filing charges against Mike, if the jury came back with the right verdict. He had a new gimmick to throw at the jury, saying that if he hadn't murdered the older couple, he certainly must have seen those that did because he was so close to the scene of the crime when arrested. He wondered aloud why he wouldn't speak up. He only took a little longer than an hour to tell the whole world how unscrupulous Mike was. Mike caught something even his sharp lawyer didn't when the shrilly voiced prosecutor went overboard saying it should be against the law for people like Mike to be discharged from the Marine Corps when it was obvious he was still shook up about the war in Vietnam so many years later. Mike watched the faces of several jurors change to a hostile face as he finished talking. Mike whispered in Plenty's ear what had happened. When attorney Plenty arose from his chair with ear muffs on telling a biblical story of a man being accused of so many bad deeds his ears had fallen off and he had asked for new ones, but was waiting for the mandatory jury to decide if he deserved them or not. One by one, he described every witness against Mike as a criminal act against a warrior of our country, a modern day George Washington, Chesty Puller and Ike all together. All of them had been in wars tougher than Vietnam if they were shook up when they ran the wars of the Marine Corps and the country, maybe they should have stayed in the battle instead of coming home. He spent some of his precious time with a beautiful description of the country, constitution, and young men who went to war to protect us all. He wondered how people could take the time to come to court to serve on the jury when the real killer of the lovely couple was out there somewhere hunting for another person to strangle to death and might be your neighbor or babysitter. He thanked the jury several times for coming down here every day to open the ears of the little man with the neck brace and his people who couldn't stand the heat. He mentioned in passing that he and the prosecutor were good friends and they had a bet that his neck wasn't really hurt and if it was, Plenty would wear it for a month just for questioning his honesty. He turned to face the audience, saluted them, turned again to face the jury and finished with a startling beautiful first part version of the Marine Corps Hymn, singing very strongly and people in the audience started getting to their feet including Mike, one man on the jury, the dainty little lady with pretty legs typing into the machine and lastly the red faced judge. When he finished there wasn't too many dry eyes. The judge gave his instructions to the jury and sent them to the jury room for as he said "A very important decision for a lot of people". Mike had a date with the detectives that afternoon so he had to leave. Everyone scattered to their own misery or delight. The attorney would get the news when the jury had made a decision and he would notify Mike, everyone other than that was up to Mike if he had time, to notify. The detectives told him right off the bat that the young man had confessed to looking in his window several times and firing the bullets at the house because he believed Mike had indeed killed his parents. The detectives stated that it would be hard to prove attempted murder and they thought a felony mischief charge would better be served. He also denied that he had been the one to try to burn Mike out, and the police chose to believe him, for now. Mike agreed immediately because he felt sorry for the young man and didn't think he meant to kill him. He had no idea this would come back to haunt him. This big bear of a man was truly softhearted the investigators thought as they left shortly after that and Mike was alone now to consider what was ahead of him in this life. He now realized what a disappointment he had been to his father when he had insisted on going in the Marines when he could have gone to college for nothing. He remembered thinking at the time the recruiter was there in the house that it was wrong, and he had actually thought at that time, how do you uninvite a Marine Corps recruiter but then again his father had always known that his son from the age of six, had been crazy about the Corps. He was the only kid in the block that could tell you how many days it was before he joined the Marine Corps when he was eight years old. Of course he just sort of guessed the last couple of days before he graduated from high school, which wasn't on the same day every year. It was quite ok for his brother to get all that he was originally supposed to get, he loved his brother and knew he was smart enough to follow what road dad wanted for him. Mike himself was always very proud of himself from the time he first went to school until that terrible day in the helicopter when he lost his courage. When he was in boot camp he met more than one recruit who were afraid of what tomorrow would bring, with the training being pushed higher and higher as the weeks went by. Even other Marines from the same platoon in boot camp couldn't understand how he felt about boot camp. It was joked around in the platoon, but not when Mike might overhear, that Mike was like the guy in the picture advertising a world tour. You know the one with the famous sights in the background, and the guy in front with the sharp suit and sunglasses getting on a charter flight to some exotic place far away. Here were some people afraid of something they had only heard about, but Mike was in a position of; bring it on. He was never let down in his expectations of how tough it could get. He would have been terribly disappointed if he thought it too easy. He had read and heard about how tough the Marine Corps boot camp was, he had read every book written by a celebrity that had gone through boot training as a Marine when they were young, and had never found one to say it had been easy. As the platoon shrunk with each drop out, it became even tougher as each man could be tested more on everything because of more time. Every day had been a new adventure but at night when sleeping, he had no wild dreams about anything because he was assured by something unknown to him that the next day would be even better. When thinking about the helicopter incident he had heard all the soothing words about everyone being afraid some time in life, but they were them and He was he and he would never get around to forgiving himself for his failure. He had never before in his life been faced with failure and had no way except strength to combat it, and it wasn't there that day. He believed in the theory of being born again after death and he hated the thought of being a terrible waste in prison in this life and is reborn maybe to go to prison again as another person. Here he was, waiting for twelve people to decide if his team had acted well enough or the other team had done better. To him it was just another way to decide, a better way than lynching for sure, or the famous gunfight in the old west but still decided on who acted better in front of a judge and twelve people by crying or shouting. He had already decided that if he went back to prison, he was going to be the worst dude in the joint. He had gained his weight back and looked good and strong, good enough to do what he wanted with other people. He laughed to himself about what his sister has said about the homosexual thing and laughed at the thought of bedding down some little squirrely sneak thief for what he was, not because of love or sex. Whoa! Where was he going with all this crazy thinking? He was stunned to his core at what he was thinking because he didn't fit anywhere in there and he never had even thought about those things before in his life. As he sat there sipping on a mild drink and now almost sure he was going crazy watching the garbage on the television when he should be doing something important, but what? Making a will? One might be needed if he was going back to prison. If he was found innocent, he might think about the Marine Corps again, but he doubted they would even take him after serving three years in prison. Wait a minute; he was employed and couldn't wait to get back to work. They had probably fired him a long time ago, who was he kidding? His mind toiled for another hour trying to think of something other than the jury. He realized that he was hallucinating almost at will. He heard his telephone ringing and he froze, Maybe if he didn't answer it would stop." Maybe it would blow up too dummy", said his brain," Answer the damn thing." "That you Mike" he heard his lawyer say. He answered with a bright voice "Yes future brother in law". "They came in moments ago but will hold off until tomorrow, nine sharp. You ok?"" Yea, thanks for calling, see you in the morning" Mike said and hung up. He notified his whole family via his father on the telephone. He asked him to pick him up on the way to court. His father became worried and asked if his car was broken or something but he just told his father "Just in case". Before getting back to the TV just as they were announcing a verdict for tomorrow in the three year old retrial of Mike Taylor, Mike prayed that he would be helped if he was innocent and be found guilty if he had indeed done such a horrible thing. He had a lot of dreams that night, mostly on how he was going to catch up on his life, and also he should think about tying the knot with some pretty young maiden, as he was finely tired of living alone. He made up his mind to sign over his house to his dad if they found him guilty. He wrote a long letter telling his father how sorry he was for not taking his advice eleven years before, but when he finished; he caught himself still asleep signing the bed sheet with his finger. Then back to the new wife. The name Kathy kept coming up. He was about half way down the list of women he knew that he thought worthy of being his wife when he heard the clock. So, he thought, this is it and no way to back out now, time to get up and dance. Mike was not that nervous, but his family was like a shadow of themselves, and his father drove very erratically on the way to court. Even his attorney seemed a little tight. The jury didn't appear any different than they had the day before, there were no big smiles but also no teary eyed women in the group. He watched as his lawyer looked over the jury carefully, pulled out a pen, wrote something and put it in his pocket. Very soon the climax started when the judge said to the jury "Have you reached a verdict?" and the little women named Junie who was the Forman of the jury said "Yes sir we have". "Read the verdict" the judge croaked. "Not guilty on all charges" she said. Well, there it was, finely, almost free he thought. The only thing now was to convince himself that he was truly not guilty. Everybody was hugging someone and he shook hands with the attorney, also asking what it was he wrote on the paper and stuck in his pocket? He smiled and pulled the paper from his pocket and showed his scribbled ; not guilty. He finished shaking hands with his lawyer's staff, then excused himself and went in the middle of big melee of his family and friends. He managed to shake hands with most of the jury before they left and as the crowd filed out of the courtroom he heard a voice behind him say "It's not going to be that easy jocko", quickly turning, he was nose to nose with Grant, the older son of the murdered couple. He was out of jail and on probation and now standing there with his brother who was trying to pull him away. They stood there almost eyeball to eyeball, Mike being taller than Grant. A momentary thought flickered through his head that he should put an end to this business with this kid and beat the hell out of him. He realized that he couldn't start whipping on him in here, not where he had just been found not guilty for murder. He recovered himself without flinching for what seemed a long time, then the deputy stepped between them asking Mike if he had any trouble with Grant, and Mike broke the eye lock and walked away. He wasn't naive enough to believe everybody was happy now, he knew he had a lot of work ahead of himself. One of the first things was to repair the damage between him and his parents and he started that repair right then by posing with his Mom and Dad for the major news magazines in the court room since day one covering the trial because of the swelling publicity across the country for the last three years. Also in the courtroom was his old boss with at the construction company, with a big smile who also shook hands saying he only had two more weeks screwing off time before reporting for his old job. Mike spent the next two hours thanking and greeting people, most he knew, some he had never seen before. He had sent his dad home and promised he had another ride. He backed off on most of the news guys because he felt it better to have a calm exchange between him and them later at his house. His brother finally dragged him from the courthouse and took him home. His friends were ecstatic, with calls from all his friends at Toney's throughout the day and evening. His family seamed completely worn out and he wanted to be alone in his own house. He was finely able, at eight o'clock that night to be by himself in his own home. He decided to call Kathy and it seemed like they couldn't stop crying as they planned for a reunion at her house the next night. She had started the crying when he had asked her to marry him, but he soon joined her when she said yes. The rest of the time they talked was about what they were going to do to each other tomorrow night amid raucous laughter. He just sat there for a long time sipping on a drink and wondering what was ahead. He was not sure at all that he could go through with the marriage if he still felt like he did at this moment, unsure about being innocence or not guilty as the jury said. Why couldn't the jury just come out and say something like; we think you are guilty, but the other side couldn't prove it. Which by the way is how it works or is supposed to work. Mike was happy, but not supremely happy, he was satisfied but there was still something missing and he knew that it was the; what if in his life. He started going over all of the; what ifs, and caused himself a tremendous headache, and settled nothing. He had never second guessed himself on such an important subject, with sports or in his short life so far. He was considered by those who knew him as extremely self—confident. Suddenly here he was questioning everything in his world. He saw himself in a day dream with his very new wife, just seconds after being married asking him if he could or would tell her the truth about the murders he had been charged with, this faded into yet another daydream of him on trial for the fifth time with his wife and children watching from the front row of the court room, smiling and yelling Daddy at him. He awoke from his nasty daydreams in time to try a good sleep for once. He was not to have any more pleasant dreams, but he was yet unaware of this fact. The first nasty dream that night started as soon as his head hit the pillow and had him up in minutes hunting for sleeping pills, but there weren't any around, so he had another drink. When he lay down again, the dream came back where it had stopped before. He was flying in a helicopter at a very high altitude when the a rifle shot hit the engine which stopped and they were falling like a rock toward the ocean when a small boat skippered by attorney Plenty in one of those sporty blue coats over a white tee shirt and a yacht cap on caught the chopper in a large net before hitting the water. There in the water was that fellow Grant with a big knife cutting at the net holding the chopper. He was sitting in a school bus and everyone but him was told to get off, but when he tried, they driver stopped him and told him he had to stay on until the next stop. When they got to the next stop, he was now allowed to get off by the driver who looked like his dad and hurried to get him to choose one of two buses sitting in the parking lot. One was the university bus and the other was the Marine Corps bus. He got on the big bus with the giant letters on the side saying U.S.M.C., breaking loose from his father who was trying to drag him to the university bus. Awake again. Like actors waiting for the cue to begin, waiting for him to close his eyes again ; Action! He was standing in front of a group of people in a large field, maybe thirty feet or so away, recently planted with tiny green glasses of vodka. It was dark, probably about two in the morning but he could see everything, and he judged the crowd to be about ten thousand. They were all calling his name softly sounding like miiikkkkeee, over and over. They would fade into maybe just ten people and they got aboard a huge bus, then come back to the huge crowd in the blink of an eye. There seemed to be music coming out of thousands of Toney's Cocktail Lounges up and down the sides of the crowd and every time the crowd disappeared, so did the bars. In the front of that crowd was the Caldwell family. She had her dancing costume on and the husband had a suit and tie but the children had leashes on, with Grant wearing a face screen mask of steel. They were all trussed up with rope and all had silly hats on. They were giggling and pointing at him when he realized he had a large pistol in his hand, and couldn't put it down. Then a sudden breeze came up and knocked him down causing him to scramble to his feet hurriedly and start shooting at the whole family. He wasn't having much luck with hitting them. Then his sister ran over to him in her wedding gown out of nowhere with a large bottle of vodka, trailed by a Marine Sergeant Major in dress blues came up on the other side of him to give him instructions on how to shoot better. Then there was his father tearing off the stripes of the Sergeant Major and throwing them in his face. His sister was pouring the bottle of vodka down his throat. He didn't seem to drink it, yet the bottle was almost going dry and he felt strange, almost like he was sleep walking. He heard himself scream and woke up to find himself soaking wet with sweat and the clock showed only a half an hour gone from the time he went to bed. Throwing off the covers, Mike almost ran into the front room and before dropping into a chair, turned on the TV. He was determined that he wasn't going to sleep again, so as he watched a thirty year old movie, probably made before he was, and tried to relax. He found it impossible and went hunting for his vodka bottle. He argued to himself about drinking any of it, but he knew he couldn't relax or sleep unless he did. He no longer drank like a normal man drinking to relax, his drinking was more of a desperate man waiting to die or finding out the truth about himself than anything. He was just getting comfortable with the old movie when he started to fall asleep, or pass out from drinking so much vodka. Either one was a relief to him so he moved to the couch, had another drink and as he put the bottle down, he heard the clock go off in the bedroom telling him it was eight o'clock and time to get up. He had no will, no strength nor any force from within to get up, almost like something was holding him down. Instead of fighting this feeling he gave in to it. His bottle had one more drink in it, so he drank it, falling forward on the couch and watched himself shooting the Caldwell family again and hearing himself snore at the same time. Several hours later he managed to crawl across the floor, he had tried several times to pull himself off the floor but was too weak. Finely he was able to pull himself up next to the sink and labor at pulling himself up on the counter enough to get into the cabinet where he found the last bottle of vodka. Was it twelve he had bought? Was somebody other than him drinking his vodka? Mike was entirely confused as to who he was, where he was or what he was doing. He had to remember to get more today he told himself as he undid the seal on the bottle and had a long drink, giggling to himself and forgetting all of the details of his many hideous dreams of last night. He had a tiny thought about breakfast, lost the idea immediately after comparing food against another drink of that life blood, took another long pull on the bottle and headed out to the morning sun shining on the old rocker. He left his bottle inside because he knew he was still either half-drunk or half-crazy and he didn't want to miss the surprise. When he asked himself, what surprise? All he got was his brain seemed to be hideously laughing at him, holding back from him what was in store for him today. He had no way to measure it, but to different points in his body he felt just about like he did about three years ago when he was arrested, but still no breakthrough on the memory problem. He knew where his medicine was, in the sky, the big bright sun. He felt terrible but he knew that in a couple of hours of sun, he would be on top of the world so he made plans for the day which included several visits to people he knew wouldn't welcome him with open arms, the Cambell boys to tell them how badly he felt about their loss. He was also determined to have a sit down talk with his mother and father on how he had misused his life and wanted to change, and with his sister to encourage her romance with Plenty. He also planned a long evening with a girl named Kathy.

    He had told his family he needed a couple days by himself and this horrible morning was finely here and he was going to enjoy himself in the old rocker in the back yard all day when he heard the knocking on his front door begin again and he willed himself to not hear it. No matter who it was, nobody was going to disturb this pleasant time off. After last night, he needed some good sun and plenty of sleep. After three years he felt like it was his right to relax at home. The knocking stopped again, Mike relaxed a little and decided he did need another drink after all. He returned from the kitchen, having had a great pull on the bottle and was about to nod off in his old rocker when he was stunned by the sudden opening of the patio door leading into the kitchen he was facing. It was in that instant that Mike remembered that he had put the front door key under his cactus plant for his brother who wanted to come by that afternoon and didn't want to disturb Mike if he was sleeping in the back yard. Who but a desperate person would hunt for a house key under an ordinary cactus plant beside the front step? His first thought was that his brother had forgotten about not waking him up if he was sleeping. The next thought was; now you are going to die, for In the doorway facing him was that guy Grant again, but this time he had a large. 45 caliber long barrel pistol in his hand. He didn't look too confortable handling it and also looked like he had consumed plenty of strong drink before visiting. He might be very drunk, Mike thought as he checked his eyes through his own bleary eyes, he looked as if he was sleep walking when he walked over and slouched down in a chair directly in front of Mike, but maybe five feet away and on the patio itself. Mike hoped he knew what he was doing even if he was determined to shoot. "I want to assure you that I don't want to kill you, but I might just wound you a little bit if you move too quickly or jump up. As you see I am not the most proficient gun handler in the world so be careful when you move" Grant nervously half whispered. He started by telling Mike that he was positive he had killed his parents and he could say nothing to make him believe any different, so don't even start. Mike was finished with that period in life and wasn't about to start it all over again anyway. Grant said he had stopped by just to let Mike know that he was going to be around every day for the rest of his life just to bug him about his sin. If Mike moved to Chicago, he was moving to Chicago, if he moved to Mexico or any other place in the world, he would be his neighbor. He went on to explain his deep love for his parents and how much they had meant to him. He told Mike how they had nurtured him from kinder garden through college and how much they had given of themselves to keep him safe. They had dug him out of all his mistakes for so many years, he felt he owed them something and riding herd on Mike for the rest of his life was what he had chosen. Mike was only half listening, watching for a chance to get the gun away from him and noticed that as he talked the gun barrel got lower and lower and was now almost pointed at the patio deck, and more importantly he had cocked the hammer on the pistol either on purpose or unknowingly. The one thing he feared now was if he accidently fired he would hit the cement and the bullet would ricochet God knows where, then again his drunken mind said; so what? Mike wasn't listening to any of the poor guys slurred troubling life story about his love for his parents, he had no feelings at all for Grant and was only waiting for the chance to close the four or five feet between them, disarm him and beat the crap out of him. Sometimes as he talked, he would close his eyes and Mike would tense up ready for the rush to disarm him, then he had decided to try once when Grant's eyes closed and now; Mike tried to leap to his feet, and nothing in his body except his mind moved. He cursed himself for drinking so much and tried again, not even his arm mussels moved. He started laughing out loud at himself, forcing Grant to suddenly open his eyes again. So, this was the surprise his mind had told him about earlier this morning. Grant was fighting hard to finish his speech even though he wasn't making too much sense now. Mike kept reminding himself to have compassion for this sorry looking person who seemed ready to do just about anything if he couldn't control the urge. Mike was not attempting to rush him even when he took off his jacket and while still pointing the pistol at him, hung it on a nearby chair on the patio. They talked almost like old companions about many things but the paramount thing was his now fervent love for his parents. Mike was happy to keep him talking, but also remembering Plenty when he had cross exanimated him during the trial where it seemed he had spent half his life being a sponge for his parent's money and time. Even in his testimony he had never once said anything that would make you think he missed his parents. He seemed too full of himself Mike remembered, too ready to blame anybody but himself for their death, but Mike was ready to talk about anything but the alternative. He had no choice anyway as his mind was frozen with vodka it seemed. He tried not to wiggle in his seat too much, causing Grant to get nervous, but he needed no worries about that as he was unable to do anything but listen. Grant praised his parents on how they had helped other people all their life, never once accepting payment for their advice or help. He was beginning to cry again with huge breaths of air sucked into and through his mouth, but needing ever more to continue. Suddenly! the world exploded in front of Mike and as he flew backward in the yard out of his chair and on his back, the sun was knocked out of the sky and came back slowly and not near so bright. He quickly realized that either he had scared Grant with a movement of his feet or Grant had squeezed a shot off by accident when he started weeping again. He could easily remember seeing the scar on the patio before the bullet hit him, and he saw the bullet somewhat flattened out coming toward him, felt the impact and heard a scream, not his own. He lay where he was and smiled at himself for thinking he actually saw the bullet hit the sidewalk, but by closing his eyes from the blood dribbling from his forehead, he saw it again, and again. He also knew and heard someone crying and yelling; "Oh no, what have I done" then running shuffling steps away across the patio toward the house. Mike was sure he had been shot; and in the head too. What would a Marine do? What would anyone do when shot in the forehead? He was surprised it didn't hurt at all, maybe he was immune to gunshots, maybe he should have shook off the incident in Nam, I mean, what the hell, it was obvious he was immune to bullets. He could feel the blood running down his neck but when he tried to think about getting up off the grass, he had no thought power and had no control over his body. Now he was no longer afraid of riding in a helicopter and could see himself firing the machine gun in the chopper. He was free from that part of his life but now he wanted to call out for help, or jump up suddenly with all that extra energy and lack of control and take care of this problem, but nothing formed in his brain, no orders on what to do, nothing. Suddenly his brain or being became totally fixed on something like being in a tiny theater, a movie started flashing before his eyes. He had no choice in watching it because as soon as he recognized the first scene he tried to blink it away, but nothing happened and the vision proceeded. It was as if there was sound but someone was trying to fix it to make it louder, with some sounds coming loud but others almost impossible to hear without straining. It was almost like a regular theater but he was the only one in there and sitting above where the first row would normally be, with the movie surrounded him and he was drawn into it and became part of it. It was the street outside Tony's cocktail lounge where the murder had been and he recognized the man and woman facing himself outside the bar. Although he couldn't hear what was said, he watched as the women pulled him back from starting across the street to get into his car and slapped him across the face, even now he felt some of the sting of the slap. He tried to grab her arms, but her husband now began to attack him and he pushed the women away to defend himself. He didn't want to hit the older man plus the guy was no fighter and perhaps outweighed by sixty or seventy pounds, but he was able to get in several non-effective punches because his wife had again gotten hold of Mike's jacket and was pulling it off his shoulders making it hard to duck the blows. Then a lucky good right hand shot from the husband hit him on the jaw and he went down, stunned more than hurt. Up to that moment he had just been trying to get away from them, but when he quickly got to his feet, he was a world away from being a nice guy. He was more than a monster; he had no control over his mind or body as this huge man was just about ready to strike out at these weakling things that had dared to interfere in his life. There were no people standing there, there was just evil. Mike backhanded the women across the face with such force she went down several yards away on her back in the ally totally terrified now at what was unfolding before her. Looking at the man who called himself Mike who seemed so pleasant when they were talking, now seemed to be a changed person, almost like a monster, when he grabbed her husband picking him off his feet and choked the life out of him, dropping him like something finished or fixed. She crawled to him just as he dropped her husband, grabbing the jacket still hanging on his back. She was on her feet now, pulling herself up with Mike's jacket which hung loose and almost off his shoulders, tried to pull him away from her husband who was lying very still on the black asphalt in the ally with his feet sticking out on the sidewalk, but only succeeded in ripping the jacket from his back, he turned to hit her in a fury, but caught the jacket as she tried to shield herself with it and knocked it out of her hands and back in the ally. Immediately he grabbed her by the neck and just like her husband, picked her off her feet leaving her feet dangling and trying with every breath left to kick him, choked her until there was no movement from her at all, then dropped her next to her husband, sort of looked around for maybe more trouble, then walked away. He walked very normal and straightened his clothes as any person would when out in public. He seemed to be sleep walking, but more than that, as if he was very tired, say after a day's work then he sat on the bench in front of a store and fell sound asleep. It was hard to tell how long he slept, but he only awoke when he heard the bus stop with the loud air brakes and on an otherwise very quiet night. Mike watched as he saw himself look at the bus, shake his head and again almost calmly walk down the street, not toward his car parked across from the bar, but away from it. Suddenly the lights got brighter in this mini theater and he remembered everything now, how he had scorned the lady and her husband just after leaving the bar when he mistakenly thought they were trying to be salacious with him for fun and games. He was standing there trying to talk sense to people he decided were as drunk as he. He had not wanted to hurt them, he had learned to like them from the bar and he just wanted to get away from them. He had decided that he was too drunk to drive at the same time as she had grabbed him and slapped him. Now he felt the burning pain from the bullet in his head, it was like a small fire with someone pumping enormous amounts of fuel on it and knew that he was almost free to die. There was nothing he could do to save Grant from the same fate as his. Mike wanted to get up just long enough to grab the jacket and gun and hide them from the police, but it was too late. Even as he turned over in agony tumbling into the deep depression of death, he saw the name Grant on the jacket hanging on the chair and the pistol on the ground beside it. He barely heard the squealing car tires leaving the front of his house followed by just the first fragment of a police siren.

The End